EL PRECIO:
The Price of Passion

SPANISH SEDUCTION – BOOK TWO

by Jean Maxwell

Second Edition Author's Cut

DEDICATION

For my boys, who are the true heroes of my world.
May you always follow your passions, as you
have encouraged me to follow mine.

Chapter One

The sound of jet engines aroused her. Zara Flynn's pulse accelerated just watching the 707 taxi to the gate through the viewing windows, its powerful whine audible even through the thick glass.

From behind, a pair of hands fell gently to her hips and pulled her close. The familiar, sexy scent of Lacoste cologne drifted around her in a comforting cloud, announcing his presence. She leaned back against his chest, undecided whether she felt weaker from his male pheromones or the thunderous advance of aluminum hull filling the window.

"Are you getting excited?" he whispered in her ear, his tone suggestive of both the view in front, and other satisfying possibilities. His wet tongue tickled her earlobe.

"David," she said evenly. "This is my mother arriving on this plane, not a shipment of two-by-fours." A knowing smile crossed her lips. Anything to do with construction piqued Dave's interest, in addition to sex. Sex with her, to be precise. Zara inhaled with contentment. In the space of a week, she and David Parker had lived through a harrowing adventure and found themselves as soulmates in the process.

Life for Zara seemed to be riding a fast wave. Becoming the CEO of Flynn Enterprises, a global construction company, was a curve ball life had thrown her without warning. She deeply mourned the loss of her father, top engineer Tristan Flynn. He'd overshadowed so many elements of her existence, from loving father to career mentor, triggering her decision to become an architect. He'd loved her mother so. And now, he was gone.

Emotions tugged at her heart as the aircraft parked its enormous nose just outside the window, bringing Marlena Sanchez Flynn that much closer.

"I know. I owe your mother a lot, bringing such a beautiful woman into the world as you," Dave said. "I can't wait to meet her."

His arms moved to encircle her upper body in a sensuous hug. Zara hadn't come to Spain to fall in love, but fate had other ideas. David Justin Parker appeared in her life as if ordained by some higher power. An engineer in the Malaga office of Flynn Enterprises, he had stolen her heart bit by bit since the day she arrived. Smart mouth and acerbic humour aside, she adored him. They'd been through life and near-death together.

Zara tried to suppress the flood of desire rushing to her core as Dave touched her. Not now. Time for that later.

The gangway extended into position, allowing the passengers to deplane. She broke from Dave's embrace, to gain a better vantage point. Zara watched the wave of passengers disembarking, and after interminable minutes caught a glimpse of a familiar brunette head coming into view.

Dressed in a white skirt and matching jacket, Marlena Flynn strolled up the entrance ramp, her Dolce & Gabbana valise in tow and her chocolate brown tresses coiffed in a sleek French knot.

Marlena looked up and waved, her perfectly lip-sticked mouth breaking into a broad smile. Tricks of her former modeling career had left its indelible imprint on her personal housekeeping. "Zara," she called above the hum of human traffic.

"Mom!" Zara shouted, raising a hand in reply. They met and embraced amid the stream of bodies pouring into the arrivals area. Marlena laughed merrily while Zara fought back tears. Dave reached to take Marlena's carry-on from her.

"*Gracias,* young man," Marlena said as she released the bag and gave Zara an extra squeeze. "*Querida,* how have you been?"

Zara hugged her mother with all her might. She hadn't expected to feel so emotional at her return, and being called '*querida.*' The word meant 'beloved' or 'dear one' in Spanish. "Hi, Mom," she sniffed, hugging Marlena's small frame even tighter. Loving hands patted Zara's back.

"It's good to see you," Marlena's voice soothed. "No need for tears, sweetheart. I love you. Smile, *querida.*"

Zara obeyed. "You had a good flight?" she asked, releasing Marlena from her hold.

"*Si,* little one. *No problema,*" she replied.

Dave dropped his gaze as he stood clutching Marlena's carry-on.

"Who is this fine fellow you've brought with you?" she asked.

"Marlena Flynn, this is David Parker," Zara said, glowing with happiness despite feeling close to tears. Her heart melted at the sight of Dave's shy attendance to her mother.

"A pleasure, ma'am."

Marlena's expression transformed from polite smile to awe-filled recognition. "You are 'Youngblood,' " she said, reaching for his hand. He took it in his palm, squeezing with affirmation. His dimples blossomed in a charming smile.

"That's me." He nodded in admission.

Zara felt a warm, burning sensation in her core. Youngblood? It struck her that Tristan might have given him this name. Perhaps her father had known even then, there was something special about David. With a shiver, Zara realized she might not be the only one destined to keep Flynn Enterprises alive.

"Jorge is bringing the car around. Let's get out of here," Zara said, tugging on Marlena's arm. They moved through the milling throng of people in the Malaga airport toward the cool comfort of a waiting Mercedes.

Jorge Allesandro stood at the vehicle's side, its doors open and beckoning in the pickup roundabout. Marlena zeroed in on him, her arms wide in welcome. He blushed and bowed his head as she drew near. They embraced, and she whispered heartfelt greetings in Spanish.

They stood this way in silence for a few moments.

Dave grinned as he stowed Marlena's baggage in the trunk. Zara stood nearby, watching the emotional exchange between her mother and her cousin. She'd known Jorge all her life, but recently gained a new appreciation of the deep bonds within her family.

An idea played in her mind lately, that Jorge might also be a big part of the Flynn legacy. She suspected a connection existed between Jorge and El Mirador, the abandoned resort property left to Zara in her father's will. Currently under major reconstruction after the explosion that had nearly killed both her and Dave, the elegant strip of Andalusian coastline where El Mirador stood, had a much darker history.

They piled into the car. Marlena took the front passenger seat, while Dave and Zara entwined themselves together in the back. Marlena twisted around and cast a speculative gaze over the pair of them. "You two look very content. Is there more you want to tell me?"

Zara smiled, but said nothing. Dave, on the other hand, was never lost for words. "Is there more we need to?" he replied, drawing Zara close and stroking her cheek with his forefinger. Zara had dubbed him 'Mr. Smart-Ass,' for his quick-witted retorts. She marvelled at his ability to speak the right words when she herself felt tongue-tied.

Marlena's mouth pursed in amusement. "Nope," she said as Jorge put the Mercedes in gear and pulled away from the curb. She winked and turned to face front, giving them their privacy. Dave nudged Zara's chin toward him and planted a kiss on her lips. Zara kissed him back, her mouth lingering on his, reluctant to part from him.

She drew back only enough to whisper to him. "What's with 'Youngblood'?" she asked as she felt his fingers tease the hem of her skirt.

"Just a nickname around the office," he said, their lips still partially connected. "Nobody calls me that anymore." His fingertips rubbed insistent circles against the sensitive skin of her inner thigh.

God, the man was insatiable. He'd have her right here in the back seat, if she'd let him; the presence of her mother and second-cousin be damned. "Later, Thunder Boy," Zara murmured in a husky voice. "Don't you dare lose that thought." This time her kiss made her hunger plain as she darted her tongue inside his mouth, then sucked gently on his lower lip before pulling away. Her nipples went hard just gazing into his striking, cobalt-blue eyes.

"Not a chance," he said, matching her stare.

Chapter Two

Ivette Melendez paced to and fro in the physicians waiting room. This couldn't be happening to her, she thought. It would ruin her career. Beauty was her business. She'd spent her life at it, styling hair, giving facials, makeovers, waxing, chemical peels, spa treatments, Brazilian blowouts. Not to mention daily workouts of yoga, pilates, and zumba.

After years of working for others, she finally had her own salon. In addition to sinking her life's savings into it, she'd gone into heavy debt to do it. Now she was afraid. Carlos had encouraged her, almost goaded her into leasing the high-priced studio space downtown.

"You deserve it, sweetheart. Why shouldn't the best and prettiest esthetician in town have the best and prettiest salon? You *are* the best, aren't you?" he'd said, almost as an accusation. Daring her to disagree with him. Daring her to be as flagrant and self-important as he. She'd signed the lease right then and there without another thought. If she was going to play with the big boys, indeed, marry the biggest boy, Carlos Sabados, she must look the part.

Where was Carlos? Handsome, dashing Senor Sabados? Certainly not here, pacing the doctor's office floor with her.

He'd been so attractive, so suicidally attractive. Ivette couldn't pull herself away from him, like a moth that stupidly kept returning to the flame. He had made big promises. Big, fat, empty promises. Behind all the flash, the money, the clothes and cars, were lies. Where was he now? On his way to jail, possibly. For tax evasion, fraud, loansharking and who knew what else. A price must certainly be on his head.

And his child was in her belly.

Ivette turned on her heel, her thick auburn hair swinging around as she did so. Her figure would be ruined, her health compromised! Her face might break out, or her ankles swell beyond recognition. All this she'd read about; things that happened to pregnant women. How could she work this way? And she must work, if she was to keep up the payments on her new salon space. Above all else, she'd never give Carlos Sabados the satisfaction of seeing her fail. No matter where he might be. *The bastardo,* telling her he'd had a vasectomy. More of his lies!

Oh yes, she was afraid. More afraid than she'd ever been in her self-gratified life. It might be too late to have an abortion. She felt trapped. She needed money.

She needed a plan.

"Senora Melendez?" the doctor's assistant called out.

Ivette spun to face her. "It's Senorita Melendez," she snapped, annoyed. The other patients in the waiting room glanced up at her sudden outburst. Ivette shrugged a shoulder and marched past the assistant into the examining room.

She waited for the doctor to finish her arcane probing and prodding. She distanced herself by staring at the bland, pale green ceiling, wishing to be anyplace, anywhere, other than this room. The hot sting of tears began to build under her eyeballs. No. She would not cry. It would ruin her makeup.

The doctor pulled the sheet back over Ivette's lower body. "All done. You may sit up now," she said, patting Ivette's arm in a grandmotherly way. Ivette sat up, anxious to dress and get the hell out of there.

"Oh now, take it easy, senorita," cautioned the doctor. Ivette ignored her, casting the sheet aside and reaching for her clothes. "Well?" Ivette asked.

The doctor paused and looked at her from behind unflattering black-rimmed glasses. She picked up her clipboard and scratched a few notes on Ivette's chart. "Well, I was about to say congratulations. You and your husband must be thrilled."

Ivette narrowed her eyes at the doctor before looking away. No reason to be rude. She may need the woman's help in the weeks to come. "I don't have a husband," she said, emotionless.

"I see," the doctor replied quietly. She made another note.

"How far along am I?" Ivette asked.

"I'd say ten weeks. That puts your due date around…" The doctor skimmed her ballpoint pen over a calendar on the wall. "…the fourteenth of June."

Ivette cringed at the thought of not being able to wear a bikini come spring. "I want an abortion," she said, slipping on her high-cut panties.

The doctor frowned, tapping her pen on the clipboard. "That's a bit sudden. You've thought about this decision?"

"There's no other decision possible," replied Ivette. "This will ruin my career."

The doctor regarded her in silence for a moment. "That is your choice, of course. What about the child's father? Does he not have a say?"

Ivette looked her straight in the eyes. "Why should he? He's not here, obviously. How soon can you arrange the procedure?"

"Miss Melendez," the doctor began. Her tiny frame seemed to shrink next to Ivette's tall, slender one. "Abortions are not possible beyond twelve weeks. If this is indeed your decision, it must be made quickly. Are you certain you can't contact the father?"

Ivette flinched at the realization she really could not. She swallowed hard, trying to soothe her throat that had suddenly gone dry.

The doctor made an assumption. "You don't know who it is, do you?" she asked.

Ivette glared at her. "Of course I do," she spat. "He's…" she searched for words that would cover the truth. "Away on business."

The doctor leaned against the desk in the corner of the examining room. "He's married, then," she said with finality. Ivette's anger began to rise. She hadn't thought about that possibility. For all she knew, that could be another of Carlos' lies. He was already married. The thought sparked an idea.

"He's an engineer," she retorted. "He's on a business trip inspecting new building sites." The words seemed to spill out of her, fabricating a story as she went along. "He's out of the country. I can't reach him."

"It's none of my business, Miss Melendez," the doctor interrupted, holding up a hand. "Of course, it would be beneficial to have both parents involved in this decision. But you have only a few days to decide. And we cannot do the procedure here. We would have to arrange a clinic in Germany and that takes time, and travel. You may be beyond twelve weeks by then."

Ivette blinked, the tears threatening for real this time. *"Por que?* Why? Why can't you do it here?"

"Because of the church. Surely you know that."

Ivette cursed silently. The goddamned church. It would cost money, too, she realized. Something she didn't have right now. She pulled on her blouse and did up the buttons, not looking at the doctor anymore.

"Please, Miss Melendez. Think about your options. There are many families wanting to adopt. Sleep on it, at least," the doctor said, reaching for the doorknob to exit the room. "Don't decide anything today."

Ivette stood motionless between the door and the examining table.

"Please see my receptionist before you leave, and make an appointment by the end of the week, all right?" The doctor interpreted her continued silence as compliance, and left the room, closing the door behind her.

Ivette considered her plan that had begun to form as she'd blurted out her fictitious story to the woman. *Not bad. It just might work.* But first, she had to find him.

*

"Does it still hurt, *querida?*" Marlena pointed to the worn-looking plaster bandages on her daughter's left forearm.

Zara turned from the car window to look at her. "This?" she asked, lifting her arm a little. She shook her head. "Not really. I should be able to have it off by the time we get back from Zaragoza." An idea occurred to her. "Why don't you sign it?" Zara reached in her handbag for the purple Sharpie she kept especially for this purpose.

Marlena laughed. "What should I write?" she asked, taking the pen from her.

"Whatever you like. How about something that rhymes?"

Marlena held Zara's arm steady with one hand and put the purple pen tip to the surface of the cast. She tilted her head slightly while scrawling her message in a deliberate, decorative script. When she'd finished, she examined her work with a smile. She replaced the cap on the pen and handed it back to Zara.

Looking down at the elegant penmanship, Zara read: *Roses are red, violets are blue. My Zara is brave, and there's nothing she can't do.*

Zara laughed and swung the bandaged arm around her in a hug. They sat side by side in the back seat of the Mercedes, an hour or so away from Zaragoza. Jorge, Marlena's cousin and family chauffeur, steered the powerful vehicle down the winding motorway. Zaragoza, the city of Marlena's birth, sat in the north-central Spanish plains. The Pyrenees loomed to the northeast, while desert conditions prevailed to the southwest.

She'd never visited before, but Zara felt permanently connected to the place. She'd been named for it, after all. Her mother's family lived just outside the city proper, but Zara hadn't met many of her relatives. An ancient combination of desert, rolling hills and forest scrolled past the window as they traveled northward.

"Jorge," Marlena said, "your mother is so excited you are coming. When did you see her last?"

Jorge turned his head slightly to the right, without taking his eyes off the road. "Oh, Marly, you know I see her every *Semana Santa*, at Holy Week. This year was no different."

"*Si*, but you know she's not well. You must make an effort to be with her more often. You will never get this time back again, Jorge." She fell silent for a beat, the next words seeming to catch in her throat. "You never know how much time you may have left."

Zara caught the emotional stumble in her mother's speech. Despite her calm exterior, she'd just lost her lifemate, and couldn't keep the pain in check forever. Mom set a fine example, but Zara knew how gaping a hole had been left in both their lives by her father's untimely death on a job site in central Java. She grabbed Marlena's hand.

"Mom. It's okay. You can cry, you know. You're only human."

Marlena focused on her daughter. "I've cried enough for both of us, Zara." They sat wordless for a few moments.

"Ernesto is getting more information, you know," Zara said. She wasn't certain how much Marlena knew about the accident. In the past few weeks, Zara had found out a great deal, enough to convince her of what she felt was the truth. She owed her mom this knowledge. "I haven't told you the whole story behind this," she said, gesturing to the cast on her arm.

Marlena's magnetic brown-eyed gaze told Zara that she desperately wanted to hear it. *Okay, here goes.* Like Dave said, sometimes you need to jump straight in.

"The Indonesian project was sabotaged." Marlena's brown eyes grew wider. "A despicable little man named Bernardo Cruz went to Jakarta. We have reason to believe he blew the place up, for financial gain." Marlena continued to fix her countenance on her daughter, waiting for more. "He was here, in Marbella, too. Working for the local government, but kept a side business called Vistamar Holdings. They falsified survey reports on real estate, devaluing them so they could be purchased cheaply. He did this to El Mirador."

Marlena swallowed with difficulty. "El Mirador," she echoed in a voice barely above a whisper. Zara squeezed her hand, wanting to say more, but perhaps her mother wasn't ready for it. "Go on," Marlena said.

"Vistamar declared the site unsafe, contaminated." She recalled the outrageous details of the report. "Then they offered to buy it, clean it up, like they were some sort of eco-saviours."

The brown eyes began to narrow. *"Quanto.* How much?" Marlena's mouth settled in a tight line.

"Two-point-five million. I said no."

Marlena nodded. *"Por supuesto,"* she said. "Of course you said no. Then what?"

"We went to the site. I called you, remember?" Marlena nodded again. "We did a legitimate survey. We thought the building was sitting on quicksand." A trace of a smile tugged at the corner of Zara's mouth. "But it wasn't."

"How did you get injured?" Marlena prodded.

Zara took in a long breath. "Dad knew what lay underneath El Mirador. Not quicksand. Tar sand," she concluded. "Do you know what that is?" Marlena shook her head. "A form of crude oil, called bitumen. It can be refined into usable oil, gasoline, et cetera. Black gold. You can see why someone else would want it."

"Yes," Marlena replied. "The fire," she said, a spark of recognition lighting her words. "That's why it burned so fast."

Zara nodded. Through much research, she'd discovered why El Mirador, an abandoned building on the southern Spanish coast, had burned horrifically more than thirty years ago. Due to legal wrangling over ownership, it had lain untouched for most of this time, until her father bought it and left it to her in his will. The petroleum deposit that lay underneath it fuelled the flames with devastating ferocity, and the original owner, Ariel Torres, appeared to have set it on fire deliberately.

"They wanted me gone, too," Zara continued. "I went back to the site, on my own. Senor Cruz thought he could get rid of me, just like…" She paused, not sure she could choke the next words out. "Just like he did Dad." Marlena squeezed her hand tighter. "I can't explain it exactly, but Dave and I, we went to have another look around, and…I felt something. I knew something bad was going to happen. Then we ran. The place collapsed around us. We managed to get clear of it. He saved me, Mom. He…" Her voice trailed off.

"Youngblood," Marlena said. "You are in love with him, yes?"

Zara faced her mother, her eyes welling with tears. "Yes," she managed. "That's how I broke my arm. We were caught in the explosion. We could have died."

Marlena held her daughter tight. "It's all right. It's over, you're here now. David is a fine young man. I'm glad he was with you."

Zara returned her embrace, squeezing her eyes shut. "Tell me about 'Youngblood'," Zara said. She wasn't aware that her father and Dave had known each other that well, and wanted to know what sort of relationship existed between them. "Where did he get that name?"

Marlena stroked Zara's blond head. "I don't know, but your father referred to him often. He seemed very proud of him, admired his youth and talent. I think he trusted him very much." She paused, taking a steady breath in and out. "He's in love with you, too. Anyone can see that."

Her mother's words were exactly what she wanted to hear, but she needed to hear them from Dave. She had to be sure.

Chapter Three

Dave felt the warm surf wash over them, and tickle their toes as it retreated again to the ocean. Sand particles shifted beneath them, chasing the water back to its source.

Zara lay naked next to him. He had his arm around her neck, and his other hand roved over her wet body. The goddess of lightning had somehow transformed herself into a goddess of the sea, appearing almost mermaid-like, with her sand-speckled skin and wet strands of long hair sticking in waves about her shoulders and chest. Tiny chunks of seaweed lay caught in it, and small beads of something that glittered like diamonds in the hazy sunlight.

The silver dolphin on its chain nestled in the hollow of her collarbone. He wanted to ask about the dolphin; why did she have it around her neck? Who had given it to her? His lips moved, but no sound came forth.

Her green eyes seemed to glow, enticing him nearer. He drew his face close, his lips grazing hers in anticipation of a kiss. He felt himself growing hard. He touched her breasts, so full and round, ran his hand over her smooth stomach, inching his way to the luscious heaven between her thighs. Another wave coursed warm seawater over them, floating the dolphin off its resting place. The dolphin grew larger. It blinked at him with steely eyes and opened its pointed beak to reveal tiny sharp teeth. Its maw gaped wider and wider, until he felt swallowed into the darkness of its insides.

Lightning flashed. She was dead. Her once warm body now lay cold in his arms. The emerald green eyes stared pale and lifeless into the dark sky above. Storm clouds roiled in circles overhead, throwing the landscape into shifting shades of gray. A bitter wind lashed at his back, and another rush of surf flooded ice-cold over them. Thunder rolled menacingly as he screamed into the wind. "No!" Like before, his mouth moved, but seemed incapable of producing sound. "No..." he repeated, the thunder's crescendo drowning his voice in any case.

She began to fade, her face growing so pale he could see through it. Everything went white around him and consumed what remained of her image. His arms clutched at the empty sand where she had lain.

"No." His voice returned to wake him from his nightmare. Dave's eyes shot open and he gasped for air, the sounds of thunder still echoing in his ears. Sweat pooled in the small of his back. Beads of it collected around his neck and trickled down his chest. The terrifying vision receded from his memory as he fought to control his breathing and his fear. It wasn't the first time this dream had come.

But he prayed it would be the last.

He stretched his hand over the empty expanse of bed where she'd slept over the past several days. Her absence seemed to reinforce the sense of loss that pervaded his dream. He could still smell the faintest whisper of her perfume in the sheets. God, he'd give anything just to hold her right now. He told himself she was fine, she was with her mother in Zaragoza. She couldn't be safer. But the words didn't help.

He threw back the covers and sat up. If the nightmare persisted, he wouldn't last the two weeks she'd be away. He might find himself on a mission to Zaragoza before then. He rubbed his eyes, thinking how foolish that might look to her. She knew how to handle herself; maybe he couldn't say the same about himself. *What a dork. I need a shower.*

He stepped into the bathroom of his small, renovated apartment. He should get a bigger one, he thought. He'd been here more than two years already; time for a change. Especially if its occupancy might be expanding soon. Technically Zara still resided at the swank Club Marbella, a resort property built by Flynn Enterprises, but she'd stayed with him on a number of nights, and he wanted that to change, too. He wanted her with him every night, every damn night, and he'd told her so from the beginning. *I don't intend to spend tonight or any other night of my life without you, Lightning Girl.*

He chuckled at how their nicknames for each other had come about. She'd called him Thunder Boy after the first night they'd made love. Partly because he came from Thunder Bay, but mostly because he'd rocked her world so thoroughly she'd felt caught in a thunderstorm. When the two of them had wandered into the crumbling remains of El Mirador, Zara gave them a running start by claiming she'd felt electricity through her body, signalling the building's impending collapse. So they became Lightning Girl and Thunder Boy—a perfect pair. As the water from the shower washed over him, his body became acutely aware that half the pair was missing.

He would have to remedy this soon, before he walked around town with a permanent hard-on for her. But how to convince her? She'd mentioned taking a vacation awhile back, maybe he could whisk her away somewhere and... *and what? Propose to her?* Jesus, he'd only known her a few weeks. How pathetic would he look if she said no? *Why would she say no?* Because she can. Because she's stressed out with taking over her father's company. Because, *you said it,* she's only known you for a few weeks.

A phrase he'd been using often lately, gave him comfort. *Just because a thing happens fast, doesn't mean it isn't right.* He knew where he would take her. If he hurried, there'd be enough time to stop at the travel agent's on his way in to work.

*

"Let me help you, *Tía,*" Zara said as she picked up the tea tray laden with a silver pot and porcelain cups, and carried it to the garden. *She's aged a great deal since I saw her last*, Zara thought. Her great-aunt shuffled with difficulty as they walked out of the kitchen. She leaned on a cane now, her gnarled hand pushing down on its handle with each painful step forward. Burn marks and age spots formed a bizarre patchwork on the skin of her knuckles.

Marlena waited for them in the garden by the round metal table that stood in its centre, surrounded by hibiscus shrubs and rosebushes. Zara set the tea tray down and helped her aunt settle into a nearby garden chair. Juliana's once flaming-red hair, now shot through with streaks of gray, hung in a long ponytail that draped over one shoulder. She'd taken the trouble to apply a lovely coral shade of lipstick for the occasion. Her graceful, hooked nose that poised above the coppery-burnished lips spoke of a remembered beauty.

Scars remained etched on the rest of her face. Her aging skin accentuated the damage incurred by a long-ago incident. Frightened by this as a child, Zara never knew how her great-aunt had become so disfigured. She wanted the whole story now.

"Where has Jorge gone?" Juliana asked, annoyed. Zara realized that after arriving at the family villa near Zaragoza, Jorge had greeted his mother only briefly before continuing into town for supplies and groceries.

"I'm sure he won't be long," Marlena said, pouring the tea. "You said you needed sugar and flour, so he's probably haggling over the price at the market to get you the best deal."

"*Tía,*" Zara said, changing the subject. "You've never told me why you didn't marry Jorge's father. Who was he? Where is he now?"

From beneath hooded eyelids, Juliana looked at her with the fiery glare of a flamenco dancer. Zara flinched inwardly. Others must have melted under that gaze in the past, but she would not. You never know how much time you have left, her mom said. It might really be the last time she would ever see her great-aunt. It was important that she know the truth. Zara cut some slices of spice cake and handed Juliana a piece. Juliana took it with a trembling hand.

"He died, of course," her aunt said, after a moment. "He didn't know about Jorge. Then he was gone." She nibbled on her piece of cake. A long silence followed, the lazy buzzing of insects and scent of late-season flowers hanging in the void.

"It was long ago, Zara," Marlena said. "You needn't ask such questions, they mean nothing now."

Zara shot her mother a look. "If that's so, then what does it matter if I ask the question? This could be important for Jorge," Zara said.

Marlena raised an eyebrow. "For Jorge? Why?"

"*Basta,*" Juliana said. "Stop it. I won't be around much longer. My son—and all of my family—deserve the truth. There's no reason to hide it now." Her niece and great-niece looked at her sharply. "His name...was Ariel Torres."

Chapter Four

"You knew," Zara said as she turned down the covers on the guest room bed. She looked at her mother from the corner of her eye. Marlena stood unpacking her valise and laying items in the dresser drawers.

"Knew what? About Jorge's father?"

Zara fluffed the pillows, her plaster cast imparting a lesser impact than she wanted. "Yes. Why didn't you tell me?" She tossed the pillows in place and faced Marlena.

"You must understand; nobody told anyone anything," Marlena replied. "We didn't speak of it. She was unmarried, and pregnant. She nearly died, Zara. Scarred for life."

Zara sat down on the bed. Poor Aunt Juliana. In those days, in a Catholic country, her situation must have been unthinkable. Her exhaustive research suggested that Senor Torres set El Mirador on fire to take revenge on his cheating lover. Was it Aunt Juliana? This story was getting more and more interesting. "Why would *Tía* Juliana be with such a man, and not make him marry her?"

Her mother sighed as she laid the last pairs of underwear in a top drawer and slid it closed. Marlena looked out the window, as if searching for something. "Zara, I'm as shocked as you.

Our *Tía* was…quite wild as a young woman. *Promiscuo.* My grandmother tried to beat it out of her." A wan smile drifted across Marlena's face as she turned to her daughter. "She was beautiful, though, and she knew it. She wanted to be a famous dancer, so she ran away for a while. She met lots of men like Senor Torres, any one of them could have been the father. She used them to further her dance career. They would fight over her."

"Maybe, kill for her?" Zara asked after a pause.

Marlena's shoulders sagged a bit. "I don't know all of what happened. But if Senor Torres caught her with another man… yes, he was capable of such actions. According to your father, he was very passionate."

"Dad knew him?" *What the hell…this just gets better and better.*

Marlena nodded. "They were close friends, he said. In fact, your father and I wouldn't have met if not for Ariel Torres."

Zara widened her eyes and gaped at her, clearly waiting for more.

"Tristan," her mother said, his name caressing her lips in adoration, "brought Juliana here, after the fire. He saved her life. And Jorge's." Her smile turned wistful in remembrance. *"Fue mi héroe."* She looked warmly into Zara's eyes. "He was my hero."

Something twisted in Zara's heart, seeing the naked love for Tristan in her mother's eyes as she spoke. *My dad, the hero.* What a love story. She'd thought of fate as a cruel jokester, not a hopeless romantic. Now she realized he, or she, could be both.

"You know what this means," Zara said after swallowing the lump in her throat. Marlena regarded her with a tilt of her head. "Jorge is the rightful heir to El Mirador."

*

Dave left the travel agency with e-ticket receipts in hand and walked the few blocks to the Flynn Enterprises office tower. He'd booked a week's vacation for two, leaving on the 28th of November. That would only be a week after Zara returned from Zaragoza, but enough time to let her catch up on her work and sweet-talk Ernesto into letting her sneak away again. Not that it should matter to Ernesto. He wasn't her boss, after all. He wasn't even Dave's boss, organizationally speaking. Both of them reported directly to Zara, Flynn Enterprises new CEO.

Even so, Operations Manager Ernesto Alvarez remained the lifeblood of Flynn Enterprises EU division in Malaga. He lived and breathed the company, worked at it tirelessly and earned great respect for his dedication. They'd worked together a little over three years now, but Dave had always wondered why Ernie, as he called him, had never married. Had Zara not been appointed to take her father's place, certainly Ernesto would have filled the CEO's chair, with unanimous approval.

Even a month ago Dave would also have applauded that scenario, for it left the Ops Manager seat vacant. He recalled being annoyed that it didn't happen that way, but had no regrets. Flynn's beautiful daughter had flown in and scooped both the CEO's chair and Dave's heart. He couldn't be happier. Except that she wasn't here, and his body ached for her.

It wasn't until a familiar fragrance blasted though an open storefront to assault his nostrils that he realized he'd walked past the Bella Spa. He'd been so lost in his thoughts as to take a route he'd been avoiding for months. The smells of aromatherapy oils and other assorted cosmetics turned his head enough to make him look inside the air-conditioned little shop. Luckily, no shiny auburn head or stiletto heels turned his way. He moved on before they could. The sharp sting of his chest hair being waxed off, flared in his memory, making him walk even faster. It occurred to him he'd been lucky to escape the clutches of that madwoman.

Dave found Ernesto in his office, as usual.

"Hola, David," Ernesto said, looking up from his desk.

"Holy shit, Ernie. You finally got new glasses." Dave smiled at him, thankful he wouldn't have to watch the man peering at him from overtop his old, outdated lenses any more. *"Muy bien, amigo!"*

Ernesto smiled back. *"Gracias.* I thought you'd be pleased."

Dave swung into one of the leather chairs facing Ernesto's desk. "They look good…took you long enough, though."A thought struck him. "Hey, wait a minute. You wouldn't be sprucing up for the benefit of a certain senorita, now would you? That would be extraordinary."

Ernesto deflected Dave's commentary with a look of impervious amusement. "I'm a bit too old for that sort of thing, don't you think?"

"Hell, no. You're never too old. *Amor* makes the world go 'round, buddy," Dave said, kicking his chair into a childish spin with one foot.

Ernesto laughed. "I can see it does for you, David. I'm happy for you and Zara."

Dave stopped his chair in mid-rotation and fixed Ernesto with a solemn look. "Thanks, man." He exhaled in satisfaction, admitting to himself that he really was happy. Really…*in love?* Shit. That tore it. He was a goner, for sure. "I wish she'd hurry back."

Ernesto stacked file folders in a pile on his desk. *"Si. Yo tambien."*

Dave considered his colleague for a silent moment. "So, I don't think I've ever asked you. Why isn't there a Senora Alvarez?"

Ernesto stopped shuffling papers and folded his hands together on his desktop. He paused in thought, as if asking himself the same question. "I suppose, as they say, the right girl never came along. Or rather, didn't stick around." He shook his head slightly, as if dismissing the memory. "And anyway, if I'd have gotten married back then I'd probably never have gone to University, never built a career."

Dave picked up the regretful vibe. "Then? When was 'then'?" The verbal slip smacked of more story than Ernesto let on.

Ernesto looked a bit disconcerted. "I meant, when I was young. I worked two or three jobs at a time, to save up for my education. I didn't have time for girls."

Dave nodded, conceding that might have been true. "Okay. But how about now? I still think there's something behind those new glasses you're not telling me."

Finally, Ernesto cracked a full-on smile. "You're a pest," he said. "Get back to work."

"Struck a nerve, did I? There is a lady in your past, then. Come on, tell me about her."

Ernesto rose from behind his desk. "There's nothing to tell, David. The past is the past."

"Bullshit. Who is she? Can you get in touch with her again?"

Ernesto sighed at Dave's persistence and cast him a patronizing glance. He leaned forward with his knuckles on the desk. The corners of his mouth began to curl. "Well, not until she returns from Zaragoza. With her daughter."

Dave's mouth dropped open, speechless for a count of three or better. "You sly dog, Ernie. You're Marlena's ex?"

Chapter Five

Zara's arm itched, and flakes of skin puffed into the air as she scratched. Grateful for the absence of the irritating plaster cast, at the same time she mourned the sickly, atrophied appearance of her left forearm. She smothered it with lotion to ease the dry symptoms.

"It looks horrible," she said to her mom as they rode the elevator to the eighth floor. "I should have worn long sleeves."

Marlena laughed and put her arm around Zara's shoulder. "You look fine, *querida*. In a few days you won't even notice."

Easy for her to say, Zara thought. Her mother stood next to her, looking totally put together as usual, her body-skimming mauve dress draping perfectly on her slender figure, its lace edges providing that so-right feminine detail at the neckline and hem. She envied her panache.

The elevator slowed to a stop. After their visit to Zaragoza, this Monday morning found her and Marlena about to enter the Flynn offices in Malaga. She hadn't been here for two weeks, and dreaded the thought of how much work had piled up in her inbox. But coming back to work also meant coming back to Dave. She missed his tall, muscular frame moving about her world in its casually graceful style. Oh hell, who was she kidding? She missed his muscles. One in particular. They stepped out onto the eighth floor and entered through the big steel doors bearing the Flynn logo.

The plump woman behind the reception desk leapt to her feet at the sight of them. "Senora Flynn!" she exclaimed, snatching her bejewelled eyeglass frames from her face and leaving them to dangle on the silver chain around her neck. "How good to see you," she said, moving toward them with arms akimbo.

"Hola Pilar, como esta?" Marlena asked, accepting Pilar's embrace. The two women hugged for a brief moment, then Pilar held her at arms length.

"I'm so sorry, senora," Pilar said in a hushed voice. "We are all still in shock. How are you managing? You must miss him terribly, as we all do." Marlena acknowledged her condolences with a nod and a smile. Pilar turned to Zara. "And you, Senorita, we've missed you around here. So many clients have been asking to meet you, I think we need to hire you a publicity agent."

The three women laughed as the reception area began to fill with people. They swarmed around Marlena, their fondness for their beloved CEO's widow evident. Zara stepped back a few paces, gratified at the welcome being accorded her mother. Amid the crowd, Zara caught sight of two figures lingering in the hallway. Ernesto held his hands firmly together in front of his body, as if willing himself to stay fixed in position. Unlike him, Dave moved toward her the moment her eyes fell on him.

She no longer heard the babbling voices in the room. Indeed, all sight and sound faded to black save for his image. Heat rose up in her torso as he drew near and she felt unable to look away from those cobalt-blue eyes and boyishly handsome features as they advanced upon her.

"Welcome back, Lightning Girl," he said with a dimpled smile, his voice low and raw with emotion. He took her hands in his. She thought her knees might give out as she caught the undisguised need in his gaze. She swallowed hard.

"Hey, Thunder Boy," she said, embarrassed at the squeaky, adolescent voice ensuing from her lips.

"May I escort you to your office?" he asked, casting a sidelong glance at the small crowd surrounding Mrs. Flynn. Zara nodded weakly, feeling incapable of uttering another word. Dave's arm slipped around her shoulders and guided her away from the action and down the long hall.

At last, they reached the cool solitude of the CEO's office, Dave closing the door behind them. They didn't get much farther. He spun her around and braced her against the heavy oak paneling, trapping her between him and the door.

"My God, I missed you," he said, his mouth seeking hers insistently. She barely heard his words above the pounding of her own heart. Her lips trembled as they met his in a searing, all-consuming kiss. If he'd not been holding her so tight, she'd have melted to the floor in a pool of desire. She pulled her hands free and dove them into his tousled locks, dragging her fingers through the soft, collar-length waves of light brown hair.

When they broke their kiss, neither of them breathed lightly. A kiss wasn't nearly enough to quell the urges seething within. Dave leaned his forehead against hers, his eyes closed.

"This is completely unprofessional and inappropriate," he whispered.

"I agree," she said, trying to catch her breath. "What on earth were you thinking, Mr. Parker?"

"Ha." He flashed his signature half-smile as he continued to hyperventilate. "I was thinking, a demonstration might make things more clear, Miss Flynn." He swallowed and brought his respiration rate down to a manageable level. "With your permission?"

"By all means, you have my complete attention, sir."

He pushed away from the door, pulling her with him. He dragged one of the hard-backed visitor chairs over and jammed it up against the doorknob. Walking backwards, he towed her across the room to the oversized drafting table between two massive bookcases. He lifted her to sit on the vinyl-topped surface, wedging his body between her knees. His hands framed her face while he kissed her, hard.

Without conscious thought, Zara's fingers went to his belt, flipping the buckle open and sliding it through the jean loops and onto the floor. She undid the metal button and worked the zipper down in a few tugs. He caught up strands of her hair and massaged them against her cheeks as he deepened his kiss, letting her continue undressing him. She separated the buttons on his soft denim shirt, slipping her hands inside to stroke his muscled chest. Her fingertips found his taut nipples and lingered there, tickling and touching.

He wrenched the rest of the shirt off, then set to work on the front buttons of her sweater, stripping her down to her lacy black bra. His mouth moved to her chest, licking and kissing the mounds of her breasts as he pushed up the hem of her skirt.

With her hormones raging, Zara felt like she might leave a puddle on the tabletop if she didn't get his dock inside her in the next ten seconds. She grasped at the waistband of his jeans and pushed them down past his hips, releasing his swollen member from its bounds. He pulled her roughly to the edge of the table, lifting her enough to free her skirt from around her bum. Her thin panties were no match for Dave's insistent fingers. Not much material to them in any case, they shredded easily in his hands. He slung one arm under her knee and lifted it to his ribs, creating enough clearance to plunge his throbbing penis into her.

Zara sucked in air at the sudden, aggressive entry, surprised at how much the rough play excited her. Her arms went tight around his back, her fingernails digging into his skin, clinging to him like a cat on a scratching post. She relished the pounding rhythm of his cock driving into her. Holy Mother, was this how it would always be between them if they were apart for more than a few days? God, she hoped so.

She took all of what he had to give her, mindless of the blueprints and mechanical pencils scattering to the floor from the rocking tabletop. Without the benefit of much foreplay, Zara still felt the rising tide of orgasm flow toward her center as she matched his thrusts.

It usually didn't work that way for her, the tender tissues between her legs typically requiring a bit more encouragement and…finesse, but…right now…*felt good.* Jesus, this was her workplace! At least twenty people stood not five meters outside the door. *This is crazy!*

A burning flush rose up her chest, her breasts tingling and tightening, while her inner thighs quivered on the threshold of surrender. The very idea of making it on an office desk, and that they might be discovered at any moment, brought an unexpected thrill. *This is beyond crazy…this is unconscionable…this is…oh, sweet Jesus, Mary and Joseph.*

She tumbled into orgasm, and so did he. As Dave was about to let out a satisfactory moan, Zara covered his mouth in a smothering kiss to prevent any telltale noise from exiting the room. His free hand cupped the back of her head. She listened to the sound of his breathing and the soft grunts trapped in his throat as he buried himself in her kiss.

Their lips parted, and he nuzzled her neck and licked her earlobe before speaking in a painful whisper. "I'm sorry…if I rushed you. Did I hurt you? I never want to hurt you. I can do better."

She kissed his cheek. "If you were hurting me, I sure as hell like being hurt," she replied. "And if you did any better, I'd have to fire you. For being so unprofessional. But your, demonstration, was certainly convincing. Remind me to have you make business presentations more often."

"Even when inappropriate?" he asked, still holding her knee to his side.

Her new phone buzzed loudly in their quiet moment, vibrating in the pocket of her skirt that now lay bunched around her waist.

"Speaking of inappropriate..." They laughed at their awkward position. Unravelling themselves from each other, Dave lifted Zara to her feet and tugged her skirt down before hitching up his jeans and zipping them closed. The phone buzzed again.

"You going to answer that?" he asked.

"Not without underwear," she said. "What am I supposed to wear for the rest of the day, Thunder Boy?" She kicked at the torn remains of her panties with one high-heeled foot.

For a change, he had no snappy retort. He held his palms up in the air. "I said I was sorry."

Two loud knocks sounded on the door. Zara flashed him an open-mouthed gesture that said, "For Christ's sake, what now?" She pointed to his shirt, crumpled on the floor and reached for her soft cashmere sweater dangling off the edge of the drafting table.

Hastily doing up buttons and smoothing out wrinkles, Dave removed the chair from under the doorknob. He looked at Zara, and at her nod, opened the door.

"Ah, David," Ernesto said, standing back a few feet into the hallway. "Could you see me in my office, please?"

Dave ran his hand through his hair in an attempt to look presentable. "Sure, Ernie. Now?"

Ernesto cocked his head to one side, his tongue creating a peak on one side of his mouth. *"Sí.* Now," he confirmed, eyeing up the two of them.

Dave turned to Zara. "Will that be all, Miss Flynn?"

Zara coughed into her fist. "Oh, yes. Have those demolition reports on my desk by morning," she said brusquely. She leaned on her desk, crossing her arms and ankles in dismissal.

Dave smiled and turned to follow Ernesto out into the hallway, closing the door behind him. Zara shook her head in disbelief. She'd never done anything so wicked in her life. And she liked it. Her phone buzzed a reminder. She fished it out of her pocket and blinked at a caller's name she hadn't seen in a long time.

Stephane. *What the hell did he want?*

Chapter Six

"It's wonderful to see you," Ernesto said as the waiter filled Marlena's champagne flute.

"Gracias," she said. The waiter nodded and retreated from their table. She fixed Ernesto with a no-nonsense look. *"Y tu, mi amigo."*

"Solo amigo?" he asked. "Just friends?"

Marlena smiled. "You know better than that, Ernesto. We will always be more than friends." She sipped her champagne, keeping eye contact over the rim of her glass. He returned her gaze with an intense stare. After a moment, she set her glass down and glanced around the restaurant. "This is lovely."

A Mediterranean vista displayed in the windows surrounding the trendy dining spot on the top floor of a high-rise tower. Soft jazz played in the background. From this vantage point in downtown Malaga, the calming waves of the sea could be seen cresting and receding in the distance, as eternal as the universe.

"Zara said you were receiving more information about… the incident," Marlena continued, looking out upon the water and sand so far below.

"Little by little," he affirmed, finally looking away from her and fidgeting with the silverware as he spoke. "Most of it you know already. The accident occurred near seven in the evening. Normally the crews would have been finished for the day, but we were behind schedule and working overtime."

"And Tristan was on-site," Marlena said. "That's unusual, isn't it?"

Ernesto compressed his lips in concentration. "Not unheard of, but unusual, yes."

"Have they determined the cause of the collapse?"

"Not officially," Ernesto said. "But I think the evidence will point to a conclusion your daughter has already reached."

"Sabotaged, she said."

Ernesto nodded. "Explosives. I don't think the people responsible intended to kill anyone. The project should have been deserted at that time of day, but it was not the case. The whole thing seems to have been a diversion, to halt progress and drive costs up. To force the sale of El Mirador to finance it."

"Ach," Marlena said, dropping her forehead into her hands. "El Mirador. I'm sick of hearing about it. I almost wish Zara had sold it to those…whoever those people were. It's brought nothing but sorrow to our family."

Ernesto held his hand out on the tabletop, entreating her. She looked up, saw the pain in his eyes, and slipped her hand into his.

"You still have family, *mi amor.* Maybe new family," Ernesto said, his voice soft with affection. His tone suggested more than one meaning to his words.

"Youngblood?" she asked in amusement, considering the possibility.

Ernesto tipped his head to one side, raising his eyebrows in concession. "That," he said, "and…don't discount yourself. Give yourself another chance at love."

Marlena blushed. "Ernesto," she admonished. "It's too soon."

He squeezed her hand. "Perhaps. But, as Youngblood said to me recently, '*amor* makes the world go 'round.' Don't step off the carousel just yet. Please."

Ernesto hoped he looked somewhat dashing in a dark business suit, his steely-gray hair smartly styled and sporting a brand-new pair of designer glasses. Very different from the skinny boy who'd carried her schoolbooks all those years ago.

A slow smile began to spread between Marlena's flushed cheeks. "Okay," she said. "I might ride it once more around."

Ernesto felt relieved that his first pitch hadn't landed outside the catcher's mitt. The next might hit a home run, and pick up the game where he'd left it all those years ago.

He loved her still.

"You know, Tristan saw great promise in David," he said, altering the drift of the conversation. "He called him Youngblood for a reason. He once said, *'Ernie, old dogs like you and me won't be around forever. We need some young blood.'* Zara and David are the future of this company." He paused, as if weighing his next words. "I think Tristan knew that. He went to Indonesia to spare him, you know. David took over the foreman's position there, and became very ill soon after. Tristan took his place so he could come home. Your daughter might not have met him otherwise."

Marlena began to look teary-eyed. *"Destino,"* she said. "Fate. He is a wily companion." She placed her other hand on top of Ernesto's, forming a living knot between them. "What about El Mirador? How can we make life from death?"

Ernesto smiled. "The way we always have. Go on living." After a heartbeat, he asked, "Do you want to see it? See what Zara's plans are?"

Marlena nodded. Ernesto waved for the check.

*

Zara wasn't about to call him back. Stephane Vanier could rot in hell for all she cared. He had a lot of nerve contacting her after everything that happened. Granted, her old phone, destroyed in the explosion at El Mirador, would have prevented him from getting through these last few weeks. But the curiosity remained. What could he possibly want?

A corporate lawyer in Montreal, Stephane had worked for the architectural firm from which she'd been laid off last summer. For a while, she'd held him chiefly responsible for the round of layoffs that left her and many others unemployed. *The rat.* One of those "strategic moves" of corporate restructure that typically did little for company efficiency but left human devastation in its wake. *Damned fucking lawyers.*

But the layoffs were only part of the reason for her hostility. Prior to that, the oh-so-slick Mr. Vanier had not only been the senior counsel for the firm, he'd been her lover. A flicker of nausea rippled through Zara's stomach at the admission of this fact. She'd been such an easy target for him, young, inexperienced and swept up in her first professional gig.

His good looks, money, and practiced charm were no match for the thin barriers she tried to construct against him. It began with lunches, moved on to dinner dates; gifts and flowers. Soon they were spending weekends at his cottage in Collingwood. *What a sucker!* Zara felt thankful her mother didn't know about him. As far as Zara was concerned, Stephane Vanier amounted to nothing more than a big, black blip on the wall chart of her life.

The worst part? She'd made the mistake of thinking their relationship held the element of exclusivity. Far too late, she discovered the string of other women from the firm that had fallen victim to his routine. She didn't even want to guess what number might have been on her jersey.

Enough about him. He didn't rate a moments' more conscious thought from her. She'd stewed about it all day as she worked her way through emails, work orders and projects that had piled up in her absence. She took a break at lunchtime and made a quick trip to the nearest *centro commerciale* to purchase several pairs of underwear.

She sat at her desk and felt a blush rising in her face. Sex on a drafting table was a bit of fantasy come true. She had to laugh inwardly at how the scene would have looked on a movie screen, her and Dave making it like a couple of rabbits in a pile of blueprints. An unbidden thought lasered through her mind and exited just as quickly. She'd succumbed to Dave's charms just as easily as Stephane's. Easier, in fact. *Nah.* She rejected the idea. *That's not true. I'm not some kind of floozy, falling into bed with every man I meet.* Far from it. It's just…*suerte,* coincidence. Fate had brought Dave into her life; and he loved her, she was certain of it. He'd risked his life for her. He made love to her like no one else ever had…like she was the only girl in the world.

Zara winced at that line, straight from Lady GaGa. She tried to discourage the next thought from forming, but it materialized anyway. Maybe she was more naïve than she thought. *Ugh.* Her stomach squirmed again.

Someone knocked, but didn't wait for a response. She looked up to see Dave's tall, athletic form filling the doorway.

"Excuse me, Miss Flynn. May I come in?"

"You're already in, why bother asking?"

He looked at her sideways, an eyebrow rising in concern. "Something wrong? *Que pasa?*"

She closed her eyes for a second, reciting a quick mantra. *I'm not naïve. He loves me. I love him. I shouldn't doubt my heart so easily.*

"Nothing," she said, exhaling. "Just inundated with work, is all. Did you need something?"

He stepped into the room. "Besides you?" he said, smiling. "Not a thing." He held something in his hand. "Do you think you'll dig your way out by next Saturday?"

Zara rolled her eyes. "Dunno. I hope so. Why?"

He laid an envelope on the desk in front of her. She took it and opened the flap, pulling out the folded contents. A travel itinerary. She scanned the print for details.

"Tenerife?" she said, glancing up to see him grinning in triumph at her.

"Tenerife, babe," he affirmed. "Need a new bikini?"

She shouted a gleeful "woop!" and circled her desk to take him in her arms. *He did love her!* "Depends," she said. "If you'll give me a chance to even put it on."

"Oh, you'll put it on. If only so I can have the pleasure of taking it off," he said, his voice dropping to a sexy growl. His hands slipped down to squeeze her bum, his fingers sliding over the elastic of her panties. "Hey, new underwear?"

*

Ernesto adjusted the sizing strap on the hardhat before placing it securely on Marlena's head. "There," he said. "That fits properly, now."

Marlena touched the sides of the yellow hat in recognition. "It's been awhile since I've worn one of these," she admitted. "Do I need those loathsome steel things as well?"

Ernesto looked down at her feet, clad in a pair of Nikes. "I think you'll be okay, we're not going that far in," he said. Together they started down the graded slope toward the shovel-bucket machinery clearing away debris and loading it in transports to be hauled away.

Ernesto held her hand in the crook of his elbow as they walked. "After the explosion, we had no choice but to demo everything and begin removal," he explained. "But Zara has this idea about building an interpretive centre. I think it's a great concept."

"An interpretive centre? To interpret what?"

"The natural resources here. How they formed, how they can best be managed. She went into a lot of detail around the technological advances they're making in Western Canada, reducing the carbon footprint and water usage to extract the oil. And their exceptional reclamation procedures. She's very excited about the process."

"That sounds like my *querida*," Marlena said, nodding. "Such a beautiful spot, though. It would be a good site for a villa. She'll need a proper home, if she plans to stay here."

Ernesto agreed. "I believe she found some sketches that Tristan left behind. She talked of building a house based on one of his designs." His next words were as measured and careful as their steps. "*Y tu?* Do you plan to stay here?"

Marlena stopped walking to appreciate the view. The mechanical sounds of excavation equipment hummed further down the slope. The soft, saline breeze off the Mediterranean blew strands of her brunette hair about her face as she lost herself in thought for several moments.

"Ernesto," she said, still looking out over the water, "I do believe you are preaching to the converted. I love this land, you know that. It's my birthplace. But my home is in Ontario. I have responsibilities there." She inhaled a hearty breath of sea air then turned to him with a smile. "But, if Zara wants me to stay, I will stay."

Chapter Seven

"Mount Teide, in Spanish 'Pico del Teide,' or 'Teide Peak', is a volcano on Tenerife, Canary Islands. Its 3,718 meter summit is part of the Las Canadas escarpment and the highest point in Spain. It ranks the third highest volcano in the world after Mauna Loa and Mauna Kea in Hawaii," Zara read aloud from her tourist booklet. "Did you know that?" she asked Dave.

A grunt issued from beneath the brim of his baseball cap. "Nah."

Zara looked over to the deck chair on which Dave lay. His relaxed, prone form made Zara exude a longing sigh. His luscious body had so many better purposes than napping. Oh well. She folded up her tourist brochure and tossed it in her trusty red Fendi bag. She and that bag had been through a lot together. Today however, it served as nothing more than a beach tote.

She looked out over the expanse of black, volcanic sand that made up the main beachfront in Puerto de la Cruz. Elaborate sandcastle sculptures lined the two-mile stretch, entries in a competition that took place on this particular weekend. Everything from traditional castles to spiny crocodiles decorated the scene, the details of each creation an astounding testament to their artists. It felt so good to relax and enjoy the simplicity of lying on a beach, soaking up the sun and appreciating the singular talent of those who wrested such beauty from nothing more than buckets of sand.

Zara looked forward to exploring more of Tenerife, the largest island of Las Canarias, the Canary Islands. Her tourist handbooks explained the history behind the name, which had nothing at all to do with small, yellow-feathered birds. 'Canarias' was a mispronunciation of the word 'canaris,' referring to the Latin 'canus,' meaning 'dog.' Early explorers found the island populated with wild dogs, giving rise to the original name.

The Atlantis theory proved far more interesting. The popular train of thought described the Canary Islands, among others in the region, as the last vestiges of the lost continent of Atlantis. The idea that she could be sitting on soil of such legend excited her to say the least.

She turned a lazy eye back to Dave, his tanned body displayed in all its sculpted glory. God, she loved that body. She felt another of the odd twinges in her stomach that she'd been experiencing lately. Bad on her, for not taking precautions. Double bad, she'd not asked him to wear any protection. But deep down, she didn't care. They were meant to be together, and if these feelings meant she could be pregnant, so be it. Fate, as her mother often said, was a wily companion.

"I'm going for a walk, want to come?" Zara said.

Dave nudged up the brim of his cap with his thumb, as he turned his head toward her. "You've got that much energy, I clearly didn't keep you in the bedroom long enough," he replied.

"Is that a yes or a no?"

"Okay, Lightning Girl, let's go explore," he said, swinging his legs over the side of the deck chair. They walked hand in hand past the mighty sand sculptures and the beach vendors hawking their jewelry and paintings. Zara stopped to buy a necklace made of the distinctive blue coral that grew in the region. Dave placed it around her neck and fastened the clasp. The choker-style fit closely around her throat, in contrast to the silver dolphin pendant hanging on a longer chain.

He fingered the little charm for a moment, looking absently at it, as if trying to remember something. Zara cocked her head. "What?" she said with a hint of a smile, placing her hand over his.

"Where did you get this?" he asked.

Zara had to think about it. With a sour twinge, she realized who had given it to her. "A gift. I don't remember when," she said, glossing over the tiny lie. Dave continued staring at it, rubbing its shiny curved surface between his fingers. "Do you like it?" she asked.

"No," he said quietly. "I mean, yes, sure. If you like it," he backpedaled, dropping it to land against her bronzed skin. "It's nice, fine." He reached for her hand to resume walking.

What was that all about? Zara wondered. An avid swimmer, "dolphin" had been her nickname in school, and the pendant a gift from someone whom until a few days ago hadn't crossed her mind.

Stephane.

Suddenly, she felt the urge to rip the silver necklace off. Why did it make Dave uncomfortable? He couldn't know about Stephane. But guessing that it came from an old boyfriend wouldn't be a big stretch of his imagination. *It's just a chunk of metal. It means nothing, just like Stephane.* Forget it. She hoped no further calls would be coming from him. Come to think of it, why hadn't she changed her number when she got her new phone? *What a dumb move.* She sighed. One more thing on the to-do list when she returned to Marbella.

She squeezed Dave's hand, grateful and happy to be with him. They strolled out to the far point of the cove, past the last few hotels, restaurants and beach shacks. The sun began to dip toward the horizon, and the sound of surf grew louder as they moved further away from the populated area.

Then she saw it.

A familiar, cylindrical building with three storeys and a cone-shaped roof. An architectural parody of a lighthouse, it stood alone on a promontory of beach. Narrow, slotted windows perforated its sides and a full-round span of windows made up the top floor. Or they would have, if there'd been any glass left intact.

She stopped short and pointed to it. Dave followed her gesture and let out a whistle. "Holy shit, isn't that one of Tristan's drawings?"

Zara nodded as if in a dream state. Yes, it most certainly looked like her father's sketch.

Los Teides.

Unlike the drawing, however, its exterior stood ravaged with gaping holes and the remnants of a bad paint job. Distinctly ugly. Los Teides. The volcano, El Teide. It made sense. This had to be the same structure as in her father's drawings, but he could never have built something so hideous. Had it been vandalized? Or, were the drawings his plans for restoration?

She thought the latter. An excitement flowed up her spine. She had to buy this thing—finish what Dad had started. "Let's go see," she said, pulling Dave along as she quickened her steps.

"Oh, no you don't. Haven't you learned anything from last time?" Dave said, resisting her tugs and grabbing her arm with both hands to draw her firmly into his embrace. "Safety first, Lightning Girl."

Zara leaned against his bare chest, pressing her hands to his well-developed pectorals. "Well, I'm not likely to find any PPE close by, am I?" she said, looking up at him through her eyelashes. "Come on, we won't go inside. Let's just get a better look. I need to see it."

"Why?"

"You know why. If Dad made a drawing of this place, it was of importance to him. I need to see what he saw, think what he thought. I need to—"

"Be him?" Dave suggested.

Zara blinked, taken aback. That sounded like an insult. "Something wrong with that?" she asked.

Dave's jawline worked a bit, as if biting back a few choice words. "There is when it puts you in danger," he finally said, pulling her close so that his lips brushed her forehead. His voice dropped to a whisper. "I won't risk that again. Ever."

The quiet tension in his voice made Zara's heart skip a beat. The strength of his arms around her sent the simple message of protection. He wanted to protect her above all else and that knowledge made her insides hum. *He does love me.*

"Okay, understood. We'll be careful. Just a little closer, please. I have to know."

He stroked her hair and released her from his hold. "As long as we're clear on that," he said. She smiled and nodded.

As they approached the broken-down structure, more details came into focus. Steps led to a wide entrance way, its doors long gone. Bird nests clung to the sills of broken windows and graffiti lay splattered against its peeling walls. A faded sign dangled from a rusted metal hanger above the doorway, the letters unreadable.

"Now here's a fixer-upper," Dave commented. "I think it's beyond even your magic touch to repair." They stopped about ten metres away. Zara looked it up and down, analyzing it.

She peered into the depths of the entrance way, walked a few steps closer.

"It's a restaurant," she said. "Or was. See, there's booth seats on the top floor, below the window level. That's fascinating." She looked at the crooked sign above the door. "Pescadore," she said, pointing to the faint specks of red paint. "A seafood place. Right up your alley."

Dave snorted. "I wouldn't be caught stewing barnacles in this joint," he said. "Have you seen enough? I think we can find a much better place for dinner."

Zara couldn't take her eyes off the thing. It seemed to call to her. The urge to possess it grew in the pit of her stomach. "Let's find an estate agent tomorrow," she said. "I want to know if it's for sale."

Dave looked at her as though she'd sprouted a second head. "You can't be serious."

Chapter Eight

The law offices of Coté & Associates occupied the third floor of an office tower on Rue Peel just west of Blvd. Rene Levesque, overlooking Dorchester square. The signage had yet to be changed, but the firm would soon be known as Coté, Vanier & Associates with the recent addition of a new partner.

Traffic noises and mouth-watering aromas from a nearby delicatessen wafted up through the open window. Expecting company, Stephane Vanier grew impatient as the lunch hour drew near. His favorite smoked meat sandwich awaited across the road. He could practically taste the mustard and sauerkraut spilling from between slabs of fresh-baked rye bread. He smoothed his expertly-styled blond hair while he checked his phone messages. As expected, no response would be forthcoming from Zara Flynn. That at least confirmed her position. She did not want to speak to him. No surprise there.

But one way or another, she would listen to him. His next attempt would be a text message with some particularly bad news. His guest knocked on his door.

"Entrez," he said, not moving from his seat by the window. The stocky figure edged its way into the room. "Alain," Stephane said. "You're late." Stephane stowed his cellphone into the breast pocket of his suit jacket. "I'm not a big fan of 'late,' ami. Sit down."

Alain's unkempt black hair appeared to sit at an angle on top of his head. His eyes peered out from beneath heavy dark eyebrows, and a wiry beard and moustache covered the lower half of his face. A checkered flannel shirt and fringed buckskin jacket would have completed the Voyageur ensemble, but instead, Alain wore a black Ed Hardy t-shirt and jeans.

Stephane chuckled. "How does the place look?" he asked.

"I email the pics," Alain replied in his colloquial French accent. "Check your inbox."

Stephane swivelled to his laptop and worked the trackpad for a moment. He scrolled through a half-dozen images, a smile forming on his handsome face. "Excellent," he commented. "Convincing. I trust no one saw you."

Alain shook his head, glancing around the walls of the office. "Non," he grunted, not interested in Stephane's critique of his work. The expensive artwork and furnishings in the room held more fascination. He sized up their value with a thief's practiced eye.

The images showed the interior of a condominium on Avenue Melville in trendy Westmount. The entrance door had been forced, the rooms artfully trashed and significant objects blatantly missing. An empty TV mount lay centered in a conspicuous blank spot above the fireplace.

Stephane reached into one of his desk drawers and withdrew an envelope. He tossed it on the desk in front of Alain. Alain's hairy forearm lifted from the armchair in which he sat to retrieve it. He folded it in half and shoved it in his back jean pocket.

"I'd keep that hidden, ami," Stephane said.

Alain shrugged. "Hide in plain sight," he replied, settling himself back into the cushy chair, in no hurry to leave.

Stephane tapped his foot, annoyed. "I'm going to lunch," he announced. "You can leave now."

"Aren't you buying me lunch, mon ami?"

"I just paid you five grand. You can buy your own lunch. I dine alone." Stephane replied, rising from his desk. "You'd best save some of it for a flight. Now go."

Alain didn't move from his chair. "That only half. Your lady friend may not react the way you hope," he remarked. "What then? I still want the other five grand."

"Piss off. You've got work to do," Stephane said, and left his office. Let the Frenchman stay if he wanted. He had a call to make, but after lunch, he decided. His stomach growled.

*

It seemed to Ivette that the elevator moved at a snail's pace. She tapped the toe of her strappy stiletto shoe in annoyance. At last, it announced its destination with a ding, and she stepped out.

The impressive entrance doors sported a giant metal casting of the company crest. She stood in front of them for a few moments before going in. The business appeared to be doing well. She hoped its engineers were paid proportionately.

She touched the sleek steel handle and pulled. Ivette's Amazonian legs seemed to enter the office before the rest of her did. A stocky woman in a red and black print dress looked up from the reception desk. She adjusted her glitter-rimmed eyeglasses to focus on Ivette, as if tuning in a satellite channel. Accustomed to being stared at, it bothered Ivette not in the least.

The receptionist cleared her throat. *"Por favor,* may I help you?" she asked.

Ivette flashed a sweet smile. *"Si,* I'm here to see David Parker."

Under Ivette's stare the woman interlaced her fingers and placed them squarely on the desk. "Is he expecting you?" she asked in her cultivated, receptionist voice.

"No. Is that required?" she replied, trying her best to intimidate the woman. At five foot ten, Ivette had no difficulty intimidating. She flung a thick auburn thatch of hair over her shoulder in a casual gesture.

The receptionist sat unflinching behind her desk. "No, but I'm afraid you've missed him. He's just left on vacation," she said.

Ivette cursed silently. She could have called him, but needed to achieve maximum impact with her news, and that meant approaching him in person. She lifted her chin and moved back a half step from the desk. "Oh, that's disappointing. I have such good news for him." She reached into her reptile-skin handbag and brought out a pen. "Do you know how I could contact him, then?"

The woman swivelled to one side, producing his business card from a multi-tiered holder and handing it to Ivette. Ivette turned the card over and poised her pen over the blank side, clearly expecting more information. The receptionist seemed to think it over before answering.

"I don't know how you'd reach him, Senora. He's in Tenerife."

Ivette smiled and wrote on the card. "Tenerife," she echoed, remembering a good time there. "Don't worry. I'll find him." She pivoted on her four-inch heels and left.

*

The dolphin spoke. No words came from the tiny saw-toothed mouth, only the chattering squeals typically heard from dolphins. Its snout bobbed up and down, as if trying to articulate a sentence by movement. Dave couldn't make any sense from its gestures. Then it opened its mouth wide, the inky blackness inside swelling to enormous proportions as the creature swallowed him.

Lightning flashed, followed by a deafening crack of thunder. Rain poured down, soaking his shirt and spilling down his collar. In the fleeting brilliance of the lightning he glimpsed her face, empty green eyes staring heavenward. Her swollen lips were parted as if her last breath lay frozen between them. Droplets of rain gathered on her forehead and cheeks. His arms tightened around her cold form. He needed to kiss her, breathe life back into her, before it was too late.

His lips touched hers in a desperate kiss, begging her come alive again. They met with dead flesh that held no warmth, no softness. "No," he cried, pounding his fist against her chest. "No!" He shook her, slapped her face. The wind whipped the rain harder against them and he felt as cold and flat as the wet sand that they lay upon. An icy wave surged up over them and as it receded, began to pull her body away from him.

"No!" he shouted again, clutching at her arms as she slipped relentlessly toward the water.

"No." The sound of his voice forced his eyes open, only to be greeted by the steely metal gaze of the dolphin. It lay inanely against the curve of her breast, fettered by the silver chain fastened around her neck.

Dave recoiled from the sight of it, bringing the rest of the scene into focus. His sweating hands held Zara's arm in a death grip, just as in his dream. Only they weren't on any beach. No rain poured down and no lightning snaked overhead. Her chest rose and fell in a slow rhythm as she slumbered next to him in the snug warmth of their hotel bed.

He exhaled in relief, blood thundering in his ears. He felt out of breath, as if he'd just finished his morning run. *Shit.* The nightmare had returned. He drew himself as close to her as he could, wrapping his arms around her sleeping form. At least they were together this time and he hadn't woken to the dreadful emptiness that usually followed the horrifying dream. What did it mean, dammit? What did the stupid dolphin signify?

He closed his eyes and concentrated on the feel of her skin touching his. The scent of her perfume reached his nostrils as he slowed his breathing to deep, measurable draughts. As he became hyper-aware of her, his body reacted in typical male fashion. A moment ago, he'd been terrified for her. Now all he could think of was fucking her.

He stroked her stomach for a start, eventually moving his hand up to her breasts. He revelled in their firm, yet yielding texture, his palm caressing the outer curve and fingertips massaging the soft brown nipples.

She began to stir, a low murmur starting in her throat. Dave smiled. His erection grew stiffer as he felt more blood rush south. He moved his knee overtop her leg and could resist the luscious little buds no longer. He swirled his tongue around her nipple and closed his lips around it, sucking gently.

Zara turned her head from side to side, her murmurs elevating to little moans. *That's it, Lightning Girl, just go with it...let me take you places in your dreams.* Dave's hand slid down between her thighs and pushed her legs farther apart. He reached upward, parting her pussy lips with his fingers to find the needy nub of flesh to entertain.

She inhaled sharply as he did so, and exhaled in a throaty moan. His index finger stroked her clit with the barest touch, triggering the flow of wetness. Her hand withdrew from under the covers, and nestled itself on his head. Her fingers twined around his wavy brown locks and she began to move her hips in sync with his touch.

His lips moved to her other breast, repeating his artful manipulations. He felt overwhelmed by the need to remain physically connected to her, as if that would stop her from being dragged away from him in his dreams. He slid his fingers inside her entrance, moving slowly in and out.

Both her hands were tangled in his hair now as his head lay pressed against her chest, alternately sucking and biting down on her tight, swollen nipples. Contented groans left her throat with each breath. He thought the sound of her rising pleasure alone might drive him over the edge himself, but he would not stop.

He felt a sharp tug on his hair, forcing him to look up. Zara's green eyes glowed like emerald fire as she stared back at him. God, the sight made him want to weep with desire. She drew his face to hers and took his bottom lip gently in her teeth before invading his mouth with her tongue, fueling his desire to an even deeper level. His dick ached with the need to be inside her.

"Roll over," she whispered, pushing on his shoulder. He had no idea what she had in mind, but would refuse her nothing. His hand slipped away from between her thighs and he twisted onto his back. She drew the crisp cotton sheets aside and sat up. For a moment, he worried she would leave the room. Instead, she straddled him facing away, the 'reverse cowgirl' move making his heart skip a beat. He watched in awe as her lovely buttocks hovered over his reddened member.

My God, the girl knows a few things about sex. She had his legs pinned under her. He was at her mercy and he didn't care. The upright head of his cock met with her hot wet pussy as she bore down, past the outer lips with their teasing resistance followed by the blissful rush of his member sliding inward to full penetration.

He laid his hands on the creamy skin of her back, caressing the fine ridges of her shoulder blades beneath her tossing mane of sandy blond hair. Her hands gripped his ankles as her hips rose and fell, gliding up and down the length of his shaft. The little bit of daylight he could see between her ass and his crotch with each stroke she took, nearly drove him mad with lust. He moved his hands to her buttocks, pressing his thumbs into the pale white flesh around her anus while she banged against his rod.

His vision seemed to blur and fill with shifting, kaleidoscopic colors as he lost control and hot fluid exploded from within him. Lost. He felt purely lost each time they were together, and each time told him with increasing certainty that he could never be without her.

The chic décor of their hotel room came into focus as his head cleared and his heart rate returned to normal. Her shoulders still heaved up and down as she too, recovered from their exertion. He gathered her hair in his hands and stroked it downward, hand over hand, feeling its silky length slipping through his fingers.

"Zara," he said, his voice a strained whisper. He tugged on the rope of blond locks he held. Slowly, she separated her body from his and turned to face him. She laid herself across his moist, muscled chest and brushed her lips against his unshaven jaw.

"Did you like that, Thunder Boy?"

He closed his eyes and smiled in wonderment at this unbelievable jewel of a woman that fate had seen fit to place in his path. For maybe the second time in his life, he felt speechless. A coherent sentence refused to form in his mouth.

"Mmmm," he grunted. "Thunder Boy like. A lot."

Chapter Nine

"Condemned?" Zara repeated. "Of course it's condemned. I can see that. I want to know if it's for sale," she explained to the estate agent over the phone. Having found the office closed when they first came by this morning, the agent had returned her call. She and Dave sat at a small open-air table at the edge of the cobbled strand, slurping shaved ice in paper cups from a nearby vendor. The African sun beamed overhead and the blue waves of the Atlantic crested at their backs.

Zara looked out over the rushing surf as she listened to the agent's words. She liked Tenerife. It felt beautiful and exotic; the lifestyle here European, yet not physically connected to Europe. The dark sand beaches added to its wild allure. She glanced over at Dave, lounging comfortably in his chair. She admired his muscles straining through his tight white t-shirt as he leaned back with his face turned upward to the sky. Her Tarzan.

"How much?" she asked, the breeze making the agents words difficult to hear. "What do you mean, you don't know?" She paused, trying to make sense of the explanation. "Well, when would it be passed inspection?" Another pause. "Well then, schedule one." She furrowed her brow, losing patience.

"Fine, what if I brought my own people in? I assure you, I have access to the proper quality control personnel."

Dave looked over at her, appearing to sense things were getting complicated. Zara rolled her eyes as she listened to the agent's voice. "Never mind. I'll call you back tomorrow."

"Problem?" he asked.

Zara shook her head as she pocketed her phone. "Apparently they can't put it on the market until someone coughs up the cash to inspect it," she said with a sigh, then one corner of her mouth curved up in a crafty grin. "Fortunately, I have the cash. And my own QC team." She leaned back and draped her arms over the sides of her chair in a grand gesture. "Sometimes it's good to be the king." She looked at Dave and smiled triumphantly.

He straightened in his chair and leaned his browned arms on the table between them. He returned an odd sort of smile; one she hadn't seen before. He swallowed hard, as if trying to dredge up some long-hidden words from deep in his throat. Her smile faded partway as she tilted her head in puzzlement.

"What?" she asked him.

"You sure ask a lot of questions."

"Yeah? So?"

"How about if someone asks you a question?"

Zara blinked. *Where is this leading?* He seemed to be preparing to ask permission to ask a question. Weird. She'd never seen him trip over words since the day they'd met in the Black Swan over a month ago. A buzzing sensation started in the pit of her stomach. *Oh. My. God. He has. A question.*

His lips parted, and the buzzing became real as her phone vibrated in her pocket. With his mouth still open, his eyes went to the source of the sound. Out of habit, she reached for it.

"M—maybe that's the agent calling back," she stammered. She pulled it out and looked at the screen. *What the hell?* A text message from Coté Vanier Assoc.' Startled, she stabbed at the icon with her fingernail.

Dolphin, since you won't return my calls I'm sorry to have to inform you by text message. Your condo in Westmount has been broken into and your vehicle stolen. As I am now legal counsel for the insurance company with which your property is covered, I thought it best to contact you personally. I sincerely regret this may cut your European visit short, but it is in your best interest to return to Montreal and attend to this matter at your earliest convenience.

P.S. I miss you. Stephane.

Zara felt her whole body begin to shake, uncertain if with anger, fear, indignation or a combination of all three. She looked up at Dave, only to find he wasn't looking at her anymore. The unspoken question in his handsome face had been replaced with a stony visage directed a short distance behind her. She twisted awkwardly to get a view.

A tall, auburn-haired creature stood a few feet from their table. Her long chiffon skirt billowed in the breeze, revealing long, shapely legs in stiletto heels. Looking like an ad from a women's fitness magazine, her bronzed skin glowed with health, her pretty face radiant. Thick auburn locks fell about her shoulders.

"*Hola,* David," she said, her Spanish accent lush and sexy as she spoke his name. Zara could feel blood pulsing in her ears and her face growing hot as she stared in bewilderment at the mystery woman. She fought back the unsavory thoughts building in her mind. This could be anyone; his dentist, for all she knew. Her thoughts reeled in multiple directions. Dave's unspoken question, Stephane's upsetting news. This, this goddess-statue appearing out of thin air. Nausea buffeted her stomach as she watched Dave rise slowly from his chair.

He touched Zara's hand, as if commanding her to stay put, while he moved toward the woman.

"Aren't you going to say hello?" the woman asked, smiling as he drew near. Dave moved his six-foot-three frame between them, shielding Zara's view. His body language appeared to be enough to make the lady step backward, away from the table.

"What are you doing here, Ivette?" Dave asked, his voice emotionless. Her glossy lips pouted, apparently disappointed at his lack of warmth.

"David, you seem almost hostile," she said. "Am I so hideous you can't greet me civilly?"

"You haven't answered my question," he replied. "What are you doing here?"

"The same as you. Enjoying Tenerife."

"Really. And you just happened to bump into me. I don't believe you."

She smiled and raised a manicured hand to his chest, rubbing it suggestively. "Well then. Believe this. I came looking for you. I have some wonderful news."

He turned his head slightly and narrowed his eyes at her. His silence pressed her to continue. She cleared her throat. "You're going to be a father."

*

Dave didn't react. He stared into her eyes, as if to flush the lie out into the open. She had to be lying. The timing didn't work. He'd broken it off well over three months ago. They'd always used condoms. *Shit. Except that one time.* In that moment, the tiniest doubt took root. *No.* She had to be lying. This couldn't be happening, not now. Not when the biggest plans for his future were about to take shape.

"You expect me to believe that," he said, after finding his voice. "I haven't seen you in months. We weren't…together… for weeks before that. Why are you doing this?"

Her smile faded and tears welled up in her eyes as if on cue. "David, why would you think I would lie to you? I love you. I never stopped loving you." She dabbed at her eyes with one knuckle. "It's you who left me, remember? You broke my heart."

"Bullshit. You were too busy waxing and exfoliating to even notice I'd gone. You've no heart to be broken, Ivette. You're an empty shell; an empty, beautiful shell. Some guys like that. I'm not one of them."

"I'm far from empty, David. Your child is inside me."

Hearing these words made his guts turn cold. "Stop it. It's not true. Don't contact me again." He turned away, only to see Zara staring at him. She stood beside the table, clutching her arms about herself as if she were cold. Strands of her hair blew haphazardly around her face and the look in her eyes sent a physical stab of pain through his heart.

She'd heard them.

"Zara," he said, moving toward her. She took a step back, shaking her head in denial. Ivette hadn't left. She stood a few inches behind Dave and put her hand on his shoulder.

"You can't walk away," her contralto voice said. "You have a responsibility, you know. We made this together, David. Please, I want to be with you again. We can be a family."

Dave brushed her hand off him as he turned on her. "Stop saying that. *I* don't want *you*, do you get it? And there won't be any 'family' because the kid certainly isn't mine." He began to move away and when he turned back in the direction of the table, Zara was gone.

He couldn't see her anywhere.

He moved up and down the strand, searching in every direction. The milling bodies offered a million opportunities for her to slip away in the crowd. *Shit*. He re-traced the way they'd come. She didn't know the area and would likely have gone back that way—unless she hopped a cab, or a boat. *Dammit*. He dialed her cell phone. It went to voicemail. He disconnected and switched to messenger, thinking of what possible words he could commit. He didn't even know how much of the conversation she'd heard.

Lightning Girl. Ask me anything. I will tell you the truth and the biggest truth right now is that I love you. Tell me where you are, please.

He pressed send.

He looked around, feeling helpless. He started back to the hotel. What a mess, a vacation gone rogue. Ten minutes ago he was about to ask her to marry him, and next she'd done a runner thanks to Ivette's untimely bombshell. Ivette. Where in the hell had she come from with that story? And how had she found him, here of all places. He kicked himself mentally. He knew better. He'd actually met Ivette here; some relative of hers owned a villa on the other side of the island. He felt stupid now, bringing Zara here. Unoriginal. But how did Ivette know his whereabouts?

Of one thing he was certain: no way had he gotten her pregnant. The chances of it were so miniscule as to be laughable. She would have to prove it in any case. And considering her vanity, the idea of growing an enormous belly would have seemed a fate worse than death for the leggy esthetician. Something about it didn't add up.

He shook his head, clearing his mind of her. Consumed with worry over Zara, he didn't want to think about Ivette. He had to find Zara, and fast. He couldn't lose her now, he just couldn't.

Chapter Ten

"Miss, are you certain you want to do this?" Jorge asked patiently.

Zara switched her phone to her left ear and held one hand over her right, to hear better over the noise in the Los Rodeos airport. "*Sí,* Jorge, I'm sure. It's an emergency."

Jorge paused for a long moment. "Miss, at least tell your mother where you are going. She will worry."

Zara rubbed her temples, her head nearly splitting with a headache. "You tell her for me, Jorge. I can't miss this flight. I'll call her when I get home."

Jorge hesitated. "That's a long time for her to wait. I don't think you're being fair, Miss. To anyone, especially yourself."

Zara frowned, unused to hearing such talk from her mild-mannered second cousin. His words showed a deep concern, and she realized how much he must care to express his opinion so openly. She regretted putting him in such a position by her rash decision. She felt awful, but awful didn't even begin to describe how she felt about what had just happened in Tenerife.

"All right, Jorge. I'll call her right now." She disconnected and hit the speed dial for Marlena's number. Zara sighed in relief when her mother's voice mail came on. She explained in a few sentences about the condo and her car and returning to Montreal as soon as possible. She ended the call, but stared at the screen for a moment. Then she reviewed her text messages, re-reading Dave's words.

He said he loved her and that he would tell her the truth about anything she wanted to ask. What should she ask? She overheard only part of his conversation with the strange woman on the strand. But it was plain enough that he'd had a relationship with her, and she wanted him back because she was pregnant. Zara squeezed her eyes shut. She didn't want to think about what might be "the truth."

Her stomach lurched. She wondered if the tall woman felt morning sickness too. Wait. Back up. She had no proof that she herself might be pregnant, any more than the long-legged girl did. Jorge was right—she wasn't being fair to Dave, or her mom, or anyone right now.

But she did have a serious problem in Montreal. As much as she didn't want to see Stephane, she would have to depend on him in order to sort out the insurance and police matters. After that, perhaps she could think straight. Take some time to analyze her life, in the comfort of home. She sniffed and shook her head. She'd begun to think of Marbella as home. Heck, she'd even thought she would build a home, on the site of El Mirador, but could Spain ever really be home?

With Dave, it had seemed possible. Now, who knew? At the moment, she wanted to just curl up into a little ball and cry her eyes out.

*

Dave raced through the terminal, dodging travelers, baggage and airport personnel. Since Zara wouldn't answer his calls he tried the next best thing—Jorge. Fortunately, the little man turned out to be something of a romantic and had no compunctions about telling Dave where he could find her.

When he'd returned to the hotel in Tenerife, Dave discovered that Zara had left without even taking most of her clothes. He booked it to the airport as quickly as possible in hopes of catching her. The departure lounge lay a few hundred feet ahead.

He spotted her staring out the big windows near the gate, just like she'd been a few weeks ago when he'd held her in his arms, waiting for Marlena to arrive. But now, she was the one leaving. He moved swiftly toward her, and spun her around by her shoulder.

"Where do you think you're going?" he asked with more gruffness than he'd meant to express. She looked at him, wide-eyed, with something like fear coloring her delicate, freckled complexion. She took a step back.

"What are you doing here, how did you—" She broke off, looking from side to side, as if searching for an informant that had tipped him off.

"It doesn't matter," he said. "What matters is what the hell you think you're doing taking off without even talking to me, or giving me a chance to explain. Is that what you do to people you trust, people who love you? That doesn't sound like you, defies everything I know about you. Or thought I did."

Zara pursed her lips into an angry pout. "Trust? Look who's talking about trust. Leaving that poor girl, in her condition. Did she trust you, too? Kept that on the DL, didn't you? Didn't trust in me enough to mention it. In fact," she snapped, "you're something of an expert in keeping secrets, aren't you? Like about my father! When did you plan on telling me that he met his death because of you?"

Her words hurt like knives pressing into his flesh. She was being unreasonable, irrational. They'd been over and over the circumstances of Tristan's presence at the Indonesian site.

She'd forgiven him long ago, inasmuch as it hadn't really been Dave's fault. Something else had to be eating at her besides the incident in Tenerife.

"I never intended to keep any secrets from you," he answered. "You know how the accident happened—we're beyond that. As for 'that poor girl', she's lying through her teeth. Okay, sure. I dated her. And yeah, I slept with her. But it was months and months ago. We weren't careless, we weren't in love." He stopped for breath, calculating his next thoughts before they became speech. "We weren't special together, not like you and I."

Dave searched Zara's face for some reaction, some glimmer that his words were getting through. "Can't you see that?" he said, his voice softening. She fell silent, considering it, but still standing apart from him. He desperately wanted to touch her, hold her, make everything right again, but she'd have to come to it on her own terms.

He had another thought. "You can't punish me because I have a past, Zara. I don't expect to know every encounter you've ever had before we met." He held up his hand with an open palm. "Everyone has a past."

The flight attendant's voice announced the boarding for Montreal. Zara looked deeply into Dave's eyes for a long moment. He hoped that moment would turn into a lifetime, that she'd drop her bag and leap into his arms. He waited, willing it to happen, suspended in time for a few glorious ticks of the clock.

"I've got to go," she said, breaking the bubble. "My car's been stolen and my house ransacked. I've been away too long, already."

So that was it. That had been the phone message she received right before all hell broke loose. *No wonder she's freaking out,* Dave thought. "What about Flynn Enterprises?" he asked. "What about El Mirador and,"—he tried to remember the faded red letters—"Pescadore," he said, tossing out every reason he could think of for her to stay.

Zara shook her head, stepping away from him and toward the boarding queue. "I—I don't know, Dave. I don't know much of anything right now. Except that I need to go home."

Home. How long since he'd been "home"? For three years, Spain had been home. Thunder Bay seemed like centuries ago. He felt like he barely remembered it.

He watched, powerless, as she melted into the throng of departing travelers. And he realized with utter clarity, that his concept of home had changed forever.

Because home could never be anyplace, without Zara.

Chapter Eleven

Ernesto drove fast along the coastal highway that led to Marbella. A misty rain swept along the Costa del Sol as winter descended upon the region. Although one of the sunniest places on earth, the southern Spanish coast did receive some amounts of rainfall, particularly now, with December dawning.

Marlena had sounded distraught on the phone. She feared for Zara after receiving an upsetting voice message. Zara was on her way back to Montreal to address some trouble with her car and condominium. The last Ernesto knew, she and David were vacationing in Tenerife. Next, she was bound for Montreal, barely taking the time to explain, even to her mother.

And David? He hadn't expected either of them back in the office until next week, but he'd yet to hear from Dave. By the sound of things, it didn't seem that he'd accompanied Zara. Perhaps they'd quarreled. Perhaps whatever reared itself in Montreal had stirred up trouble between the couple. *That would be a shame,* he thought.

He had an inkling that David was about to pop the question to Zara while they were away. Though Ernesto would normally have recommended a long, slow courtship, he could see that these young people didn't operate that way. And he didn't mind. The two were made for each other. In fact, the sooner Zara and David were together permanently, the better for everyone and everything. Like the company succession plan.

With Tristan gone, Ernesto had been prepared to take on the CEO position if called upon. He and Tristan had more or less built the company together. Tristan made no secret of the fact that Ernesto played the part of right-hand man. But in the end, he chose his daughter as his replacement. And David seemed the perfect partner for her. Ernesto saw great things in their future together.

And what of his own future? Retirement loomed not far off. The company would be in good hands, and for the last several weeks, Ernesto sensed that his future lay inextricably linked to his past. A past that waited in her suite at Club Marbella.

Oh, she had been so lovely, that chocolate-haired girl from the edge of the city. He saw her arrive at school on the bus each day, and their friendship grew from carrying her books to joining the drama and citizenship clubs together. They'd worked in the orchards during the summer for extra pay and watched the stars at night.

And then one day, Tristan arrived with Marlena's aunt in tow. It wasn't surprising that he swept her off her feet. Blond, handsome and fearless, Tristan set the whole community on its ear in admiration of him, Ernesto included. He was just that sort of man, the conquering hero who flew into town with his imaginary cape flapping behind him.

When Ernesto left to study engineering at the University in Madrid, Tristan had already been forming Flynn Enterprises and insisted that Ernesto return and work for him upon graduation. The rest, as is often said, is history. He'd never worked for another firm. It was no wonder Ernesto cared for and shepherded the company so stalwartly.

And he'd accepted that Marlena chose to marry Tristan. Life went on, and on. And now, thirty years later, Ernesto found himself driving on a rain-soaked motorway, on his way to her. What was that turn of phrase she liked to use? Oh, yes. *Fate is a wily companion.*

He parked his car and entered through the grand doors of Club Marbella. His eyes scanned the opulent lobby, with its massive ceiling fans and lush upholstery gracing the huge expanse of marble tile and glittering lights. Marlena stood near the indoor fountain, surrounded by exotic plants, looking like a graceful water bird perched on its stony edge. She caught sight of him, and walked toward him. Ernesto had never seen her look so needful. And perhaps because of this, to him, she never looked more beautiful.

He scooped her into his arms in a protective hug, wishing it were more, yet needing to uphold the position of friendship they'd built over so many years. "Marly," he said, "It's going to be all right, I'm here now."

"I know," she said, returning his squeeze. "I've tried calling her, but she must still be in flight. I've left voice messages. I don't know what's going on."

"Does she have someone to meet her when she lands?" Ernesto asked.

Marlena's head moved side to side. "I imagine she'll take a taxi, but if her condo's been really damaged, or sealed by police, she might not be able to stay there. I'm not sure where she'll go. Barrie is too far from Montreal."

"Well, I'm sure she'll call when she gets there," Ernesto assured her. "Where is Jorge? He might know something."

Marlena nodded. "The Mercedes is gone. He must be out doing errands." She wiped the corner of her eye with one finger, drawing back from Ernesto's embrace. "But where is David? Have you heard from him?"

Ernesto shook his head. "Not yet. It doesn't sound like he went with her. They weren't due back from Tenerife until Sunday. He might still be there." He had no other words of comfort, but had to do something. "Come, let's get something to eat, a coffee at least," he said, guiding her towards the hotel bar.

She sighed then nodded. She reached for Ernesto's hand as they started across the marble floor together, when she glanced over at the entrance, stopping short. A damp Jorge came walking in, brushing the rain off his jacket. He spotted Marlena, and moved to join them.

"Jorge," Marlena exclaimed, the relief in her voice evident. *"Que pasa, como esta Zara y David?"*

Jorge took out a handkerchief and wiped the moisture from his face. "She boarded the flight to Montreal safely," he assured them. "She promised to call you. Did you receive her message?"

Marlena nodded. *"Si,* but she didn't explain much. Who broke into her house? Is someone meeting her in Montreal? What did she say to you? Did David go with her?"

Jorge pocketed his handkerchief. "She got a message from a lawyer with the insurance company. He told her that the apartment had been turned upside down and her car stolen. He advised her to return to Montreal as soon as possible."

Ernesto and Marlena looked at him, their expressions clearly wanting more. "David is not with her," he continued. "He called me. Something happened between them, she left suddenly after receiving the news from the lawyer. He lost sight of her. She had already called me, asking to let you know." He managed an apologetic grin. "I told him where to find her at the airport."

Marlena looked between the two men. "So he might be with her, we don't know," she said. She shook her head and cursed in Spanish. Ernesto raised an eyebrow at her uncharacteristic burst of expletives. Jorge shrugged.

"There's nothing to do but wait. We might as well eat, then," Marlena said, resigned. "Or drink. I think I could use a drink," she decided, nodding. She looked between the two men, who stood before her both gaping in surprise. She waved her hand impatiently. *"Vamos, mi muchachos."*

*

"Monsieur Vanier," the hostess said. "This way, please."

Stephane tossed the GQ magazine he'd been reading onto a cocktail table, and rose from his chair to follow the hostess into the treatment area. A massage bed lay waiting for him behind a partition.

Damn, air travel has come a long way, he thought, slipping off his shoes. The airport at Dorval now boasted a drop-in massage studio for the convenience of travellers with long stopovers. The hostess held out her hands for his jacket and tie. This studio didn't offer the kind of full massage he might have preferred, but since he had to wait anyway, he might as well be pampered to the extent a public facility would allow.

He lay face down on the bed while the masseuse worked her magic on his back.

So far, so good. Zara was on her way to Montreal, the flight due within the hour. He would be waiting for her in his polished, lawyer-ish demeanor, ZZegna suit and Nunn Bush footwear. He hoped he hadn't put on too much weight since she'd seen him last. The first impression had to be spot-on.

First, her condo. Alain had rendered it unlivable for the moment, necessitating her accommodations elsewhere. Stephane's house would be generously offered for her use during her stay. In a display of chivalry, he would insist that he himself stay elsewhere, knowing her current dislike for him.

But this would change by week's end. Stephane rarely did not achieve what we wanted.

Next, her BMW would miraculously turn up, undamaged, thanks to Stephane's dogged investigation of the theft. Her gratefulness would know no bounds. Until then, he would graciously supply her with whatever transportation she desired.

Then, with a few phony claims papers signed, he would help her shop for new furnishings and hire contractors to redecorate her home in impeccable style. By that time, the holidays would be nearly upon them and his Collingwood cottage, a perfect festive retreat, would beckon for a Christmas getaway.

Somewhere in that mix, he would broach the topic of the Flynn Enterprises Montreal office. The financial reports were a mess. Staff turnover had left the place nearly deserted and project bids had come to a standstill. Or so it would seem. And to the rescue, Stephane Vanier would step in, posted by acclamation to the Board of Directors of Flynn Enterprises North America, and save the day.

He sighed with gratification, as if he'd just watched the whole plan play out on a movie screen. Or perhaps it was the expert manipulations of the masseuse who worked on his lower back, hitting precisely the exact vertebrae that drew satisfied moans from his lips. Perhaps the girl would be looking for a date later on. He turned his head to get a glimpse of her.

A large, East Indian woman bent over him, the muscles in her arms flexing and bulging as she worked. Nope, he thought, observing her heavy black eyebrows with a red dot painted between them. While he wasn't averse to a little brown sugar from time to time, this lady held no appeal for him at all. He turned his face back into the pillow, taking care not to muss his hair.

He pondered the severity of Zara's feelings toward him. Had she softened her attitude at all since her layoff? Bygones were bygones. And though he knew she blamed him for the corporate bloodletting, it wasn't completely his doing. The firm had financial difficulties. The quickest way to cut the budget was to cut staff. Owners understood this, but employees rarely did. The Montreal operation would be no different, a rational, expedient course of action. He didn't handpick those who were to be let go. It was 'last in, first out' like any other business decision. Zara had simply been there the least amount of time. *Well,* he smirked, *her and a hundred others.*

But for one of the first times, his plan hadn't gone exactly his way. She disappeared so quickly she simply hadn't allowed him the opportunity to play the hero, offer her another job, a better job, with a law firm he was soon to partner with.

During the course of their relationship, she'd told him how strongly she felt about not working for her father at Flynn Enterprises. Now, however, it appeared she had accepted the big prize, taking over the European division of the company. Perhaps she'd have a bigger interest in the company now, as a whole, and allow him to proceed with his takeover of the North Am branch.

He checked his watch. The masseuse had finished with him, placing a hot towel over his back and leaving the room. 30 minutes to touchdown. He really did like Zara. She was pretty, and smart. He liked those qualities, although not always a requirement for the ladies in his entourage. But Zara offered something the others did not. Something he wanted, besides sex. He smiled outright, imagining he must look like the Grinch the day before Christmas.

She offered opportunity.

*

Ivette flopped down on a chaise lounge, looking out at the ocean. The terrace of her uncle's villa provided a comfortable refuge from the inner turmoil she felt. Things hadn't gone as well as planned. David had been undeniably displeased at her reappearance in his life.

She almost felt sorry for the little blondish wisp of a girlfriend he'd brought along. He'd have some fast talking to do if he hoped to salvage that relationship. But it made no difference to Ivette. If David had been responsive to her offer, she'd have gladly resumed their affair, even if it meant living a lie. Handsome and funny, she truly did like the man. He'd make a suitable husband, even if he wasn't a big-leaguer like Carlos.

But no matter. All she had to do was push him beyond his guilt threshold and make him pay. He might even feel lucky, to extricate himself from an unfavorable situation merely by parting with a few thousand euro.

There did remain a problem, though. She had no intention of becoming a mother. She found the very idea abhorrent; the ravaging of her perfect body, the existence of a completely needy little being that would consume her every action and thought for years to come. And how difficult to attract another suitor with an infant on the scene? No. This just wouldn't work for her.

The doctor said the procedure couldn't be done after twelve weeks, but Ivette had read otherwise. A therapeutic abortion couldn't be performed, but there were other methods, and other doctors. Both of which cost money. Ivette snorted in frustration, throwing a pebble over the railing of the terrace onto the beach below. *Carlos, where are you?* she fretted. If only he wasn't running from the law, life could have been so rosy for both of them. *Damn him.*

She'd have to give Dave one more try. Maybe after he'd had a chance to think about it, acknowledge the possibility he could be the father, he might feel differently. He had a conscience, unlike many men. If that failed, there remained the legal avenue; serve him with papers and a proposal for financial settlement.

She wondered how long she should wait. Her trip to Holland for medical treatment should be booked as soon as possible, but she had to secure her financial position first. She gave herself two weeks, three at most, to complete everything. With any luck, she'd be serving her first customer in her beautiful new salon, worry-free, by New Years'. That's it, she thought; a New Years' party. A celebration of her new business and her new life would be the hit of the season. The thought made her smile, despite the unpleasantness ahead.

Chapter Twelve

Ernesto returned to the office. By the time he finished lunch with Marlena and driven back to Malaga, the wall clock in the reception area read five fifteen p.m. Pilar and the other staffers had already left. A good thing, anyway. He didn't really want to deal with any people at the moment.

He picked up a stack of mail from his inbox and proceeded to the hallway leading to his office. Treading silently down the carpeted corridor, he heard faint music behind him. He stopped and did an about face. The door to David's office stood open and soft guitar sounds emanated from it. He strode toward it, anxious to see Dave and hear his version of events.

Peering across the threshold, Ernesto spotted Dave reclining in his office chair, the acoustic guitar that normally sat in a stand in the corner resting in his lap. Dave held the instrument in such a way it made Ernesto imagine Zara in its place. Dave's hands caressed it lovingly, gently striking its strings and sliding his fingers along the fret board. His eyes were closed and he seemed to be picking out a tune from memory, losing himself in the melody and whatever personal meaning the song held for him.

Ernesto hung back, appreciating the pensive mood in the room for a few moments. When the last note sounded, followed by silence, Ernesto cleared his throat to announce his presence. Dave's eyes snapped open and bolted upright in his chair.

"Jesus, Ernie, you could have knocked."

"And you could have called," Ernesto remarked, leaning against the door frame and crossing one foot over the other. He smiled a fatherly smile. *"Que pasa, mi hijo?"* he asked in a quiet voice. He realized he had actually come to regard Dave as a son, of sorts.

Dave took a deep breath and swung the guitar out of his lap and back onto its stand. "I love this place so much I couldn't stay away."

"I doubt that," Ernesto said. After experiencing Dave's sense of humour all these years, he understood the trait was also the young man's method of coping under stress. "But if that's all you want to say, I understand."

Dave tilted back in his chair again and studied the ceiling, not looking at Ernesto. "I have a lot to say," he began. "But the person that needs to hear it isn't here."

"And why is that?" pressed Ernesto.

"She had personal business in Montreal."

"That much I heard. Why aren't you with her?"

"She's angry with me." He rocked his chair back and forth a few times. "And come to think of it, I'm angry with myself."

Ernesto said nothing, letting Dave get out whatever he was going to get out. Dave turned to face him. "I've let something from my past jeopardize my future." A pointed look from Ernesto made him continue. "Do I have a future here, Ernie? I've put in my time. With a new CEO at the helm, and you still years away from retirement, maybe there's no place for me here anymore. Maybe I should move on."

That spurred Ernesto into action. He stepped into the room and drew up a chair across the desk from Dave. "I won't allow that kind of talk," he said, seating himself. "You and Zara are the future of this company. Tristan as much as said so. What the devil is going on in your head? I can't help you if you won't tell me."

Dave winced as if in almost physical pain. "I'm in love with her, Ernie. That's not a good business plan."

"To use your word, David…bullshit." Dave's eyebrows went up. "It's the perfect business plan," Ernesto continued. "There's no stronger foundation for an organization than family. No one could care more about this company than the two of you. And soon,"—he tapped his index finger on the desk—"there'll be a whole new generation of family to carry it on. I'm sure of it."

At Ernesto's last words, Dave looked as if he were about to choke. He put his hands to his forehead and dropped his face to his desk. "Oh, Ernie," he said. "I've screwed up."

"Why? What are you trying to say?"

"I may already be a father. A surprise visitor turned up in Tenerife; someone I knew…before. She says she's pregnant. She says it's mine."

Ernesto felt Dave's anguish from across the desk. He looked steadily at him, thinking what "fatherly" advice he might offer. No pun intended. "And Zara heard this?" he asked. Dave nodded. "Well." Ernesto said. "Number one, is it possible? Number two, can she prove it? Number three, do you still have feelings for this woman?"

"Yes, maybe and no."

"Go on."

"Yes, it's theoretically possible, but highly unlikely. I've no idea how she'd prove it. Or how I could disprove it, for that matter. And the only feelings I have for her at the moment all start with the letter R. Rage, remorse and repugnance. Not to mention regret."

Ernesto let out a low whistle. "That's a lot of emotions. And what did Zara say?"

"Nothing. She took off. I chased her all the way to the airport before I could get her to talk to me. I told her everything. I didn't want any secrets between us. For a minute, I thought she'd change her mind and stay, but her apartment's been broken into and her car stolen. She got a message from someone right before—" Dave broke off. "She's got a lot on her mind right now. And she's homesick. I had to let her go." He looked out the window.

Ernesto rubbed his chin, thinking. "You're right. She has to make her own decisions. It sounds like she just needs some space."

Dave snorted. "There's a hell of a lot of space between here and Montreal."

Ernesto nodded. *"Si,* but give her some time, a few days or so. Then I suggest you close that space."

"You think I should go after her?"

Ernesto smiled. "David, for as long as I've known you, you've always gone after what you wanted. Don't stop now."

*

Snow. Pellets of snow whipped past the aircraft windows at an angle, driven by a bitter wind. How long since she'd seen snow? She didn't even have proper clothes for this weather. Zara reached for her Fendi bag stowed under the seat in front of her, preparing to disembark. In a window seat in row thirty-four, she'd be a while yet. She sighed and folded the bag on her lap. Her phone buzzed inside it.

She fished it out and read the screen. Stephane's text message said:

Welcome home, I'm waiting for you at the gate.

Zara's stomach flipped a bit. Had there been some other way to conduct her business here, without having to lay eyes on the man, she'd have done it. But for expediency, she had to take Stephane at his word and accept the help he offered. It would be the quickest way to assess the damage and get the insurance wheels in motion.

She bit her lip, a sick stab of regret striking her insides at the thought of her condo in ruins. Perhaps the damage wouldn't be as bad as Stephane made it sound. Walls were repairable, furniture replaceable, but her car was still missing, and that bothered her even more. Stolen cars were rarely recovered intact. She feared the worst for her poor BMW.

At last, she stood and maneuvered her way into the aisle. She reached into the overhead bin for her carry-on and followed the line of fellow passengers moving ahead. She felt exhaustion about to overtake her. She'd never mastered the art of sleeping on airplanes. She loved flying in them, but could never sleep on them. Stephane said he would arrange her accommodations. Sadly, she could not stay in her own home. She hoped he'd booked a decent hotel. She'd kick his ass if he hadn't. Though fundamentally a cad, the man did have taste. She suspected the hotel would be the least of her worries.

She trudged up the ramp, the grating whine of tiny luggage wheels reverberating in her ears and the bland odor of recirculated air filling her nose. She kept her head down as she entered the arrivals area, her eyes drawn to the fleur-de-lis pattern on the carpet. She felt bone-tired. Suddenly, her luggage was lifted from her grip. Startled into alertness, she followed the vision of the immaculately manicured hand that had caught hold of the handle, then upward past the suit-jacketed arm and the broad shoulders that stooped over her bag.

Stephane's blond head tipped up, bringing his face into full view just inches away from hers. He looked every bit the lawyer she remembered. If anything, an added year or so only increased his attractiveness. He looked…distinguished.

Though her loathing remained undiminished, staring point-blank into his chiselled features made her recall all too clearly how she'd fallen for the dirtbag in the first place. The alluring aroma of Hugo Boss exuded from him.

"Bonjour, Dolphin," he said in that rumbling baritone she'd stored away in the archives of her memory banks. A bedroom voice. Guaranteed to melt female knees at twenty paces. "Let me get that for you." Stephane straightened to his full height. "You look wonderful," he said. "The Mediterranean lifestyle must agree with you. Bad news, though. It's snowing outside."

Zara looked at him blankly. "Yeah, I noticed."

Stephane smiled. "I've bought you something." He offered out a large Holt-Renfrew shopping bag. Zara looked at him with suspicion, but gingerly lifted the handles of the bag from his outstretched fingers. Rather heavy, she sat it on the floor and withdrew its contents.

She couldn't help but draw in a sudden breath as she handled it, a cape with black fur trim at the collar and hem, the fabric a deep, purple shearling brocade. Its beautiful texture rippled in the fluorescent lighting overhead. *It must have cost thousands*, Zara thought. As much as she wanted to put it on, it smacked of bribery. "I can't accept this."

"Oh, now, be practical, Dolphin. It's cold out, and I can tell by your luggage you've no winter clothes with you. Put it on. It'll be more beautiful with you wearing it."

Zara's tongue went thick inside her mouth, his flattering words having the same effect as eating a spoonful of honey. He tilted his head and took the elegant garment from her. With a chivalrous swoop, he landed it about her shoulders and snuggled the warm fur collar under her chin.

"There. A Snow Queen," he pronounced.

"I'd like to see my condo, please," Zara said, declining to express thanks.

"Of course. Let's go." Stephane began moving them through the busy terminal. As they stepped outdoors, the bitter wind struck Zara full force. She'd nearly forgotten about winter in her busy few months in Spain, but it made its presence known all too vividly now. She felt grateful for the luxurious cloak around her, though not quite enough to say so.

Stephane's Jaguar sat parked in a VIP zone nearby. Its sleek silver exterior shining even in the snowy gloom. Once upon a time, this car, as well as Stephane's many other toys and luxuries, had impressed her. Now they just came off as pretentious. As he opened the door for her, some long-forgotten words sing-songed in her head.

"Come into my parlor, said the spider to the fly."

Zara hesitated at the curb, staring into the gray interior that threatened to swallow her.

"Something wrong?" Stephane asked.

I'm being silly. It's a car, nothing more. Wheels and an engine. That's it. She shook her head and slid into the leather bound luxury of the passenger seat.

Stephane strode to the drivers side and got behind the wheel. "Buckle up, baby." She'd barely clicked the thing in place before the Jag seemed to throw a couple of G's as he peeled away from the curb.

Chapter Thirteen

The tree-lined street seemed magical, yet foreign in its powder-coating of snow. It didn't look like the neighborhood she remembered, but soon Zara's stately brick four-plex came into view and tripped an unexpected flutter of joy in her heart. She'd come home.

Stephane pulled up at the building's entrance. An arched portico framed the twin front doors, their enamelled red finish gleaming in the wintry light. The caretakers had placed a holly wreath on each one. Everything looked normal from the outside.

Her suite occupied the upper west side of the building. Zara could see her bedroom bay window from the front. She and Stephane walked the stone steps of the veranda to stand before the red doors.

"You have your key," he said, not as a question, but as a statement.

Zara reached into her bag and produced a keychain without comment. The unlocked red doors led into a broad vestibule, decorated in greens and burgundies. An antique mailbox with four compartments stood off to one side, opposite an upholstered slipper chair and round side table. An elegant oval rug covered the floor and a cheery holiday arrangement of cedars and berries topped the little table's polished surface.

"Nice," Stephane commented.

Zara ignored the mailbox and pushed her key into the deadbolt of the inner door. With a twist, the bolt released, and Stephane's hand was upon the handle before Zara could even remove the key. She allowed him to open it for her.

"You won't be happy with what you're about to see," he said, moving close as to put an arm around her. Zara moved forward, away from his reach, and started up the stairs. The sound of her steps on the burnished hardwood treads brought back the memories of a life she'd lived seemingly aeons ago. She dreaded what might await her at the second floor landing.

Turning left at the top of the staircase, her door stood chipped and gouged around the doorknob, where someone had forced their way in. A realtor's lockbox held a temporary latch in place. Stephane had the key for it and removed the heavy padlock. He pushed the door wide for her to enter.

Crossing the threshold, Zara couldn't stifle a gasp as she beheld the dishevelled mess that had been her home. She saw her desk overturned with one leg sheared off, couch cushions ripped and thrown about the room. Not a single piece of electronics remained, the most conspicuous being the flatscreen that no longer occupied the space above the fireplace.

Kitchen drawers lay piled haphazardly atop one another on the floor, their contents strewn across the tiled surface.

Shattered dishes littered the sink, cabinet doors hung open at various angles. She covered her mouth with her hand, feeling her stomach writhe in anguish at the sight. She moved to the bedroom, picking her way across the devastated living space. Her Tiffany floor lamp lay horizontal in her path, its stained-glass shade broken beyond repair. With regret, she stepped over it.

Her bed. Why someone would desecrate her bed in such a way was unfathomable. The mattress lay shoved off the bed frame, and propped against the window. Pillows were thrown to corners of the room and broken items from her nightstand tossed onto the box spring. And covering it all, a mass of feathers from her down comforter that lay torn to shreds at her feet.

Zara began to sob aloud. She felt her life coming apart in two places, first in Tenerife, and now here in Montreal. What had she done to deserve this? Her shoulders slumped beneath the luxurious purple cape, all resistance seeming to have drained from her body. This was too much to bear. She closed her eyes and wished for it all to be a bad dream, and to wake up with Dave's arms around her.

"You're exhausted," Stephane's deep but soft voice said. He stood close behind her, his tall, solid form lending a physical presence that swept over her like a warm breeze. In her despair, she suddenly felt like melting into it, to admit defeat and simply lean on this rock-wall of a man that she despised.

His hands came to rest on her arms, exerting a gentle pressure that Zara felt too despondent to resist. "I think you've seen enough, Dolphin. I'm so sorry. Let me take you out of here and buy you dinner. You must be starving." He tightened his grip and motioned her to turn around. She had no fight left in her. She moved like a zombie, letting him guide her back through the chaos and out the door.

"I'm not hungry," she grumbled.

"I thought you might say something like that. Trust me, you need food."

"I need rest, not food."

"Fine, we'll get you some rest, and then some food. Either way you're going to eat. Just let me take care of you." Keeping his hold on her, they walked to the staircase and began to descend.

Zara had no intention of allowing this callous beast to take care of her. "I can take care of myself," she said, her shoes plonking on each of the treads.

"Sure you can. But for once, let someone else do it. Just this time, okay? I'd never forgive myself if I left you alone in such a state."

Zara snorted a laugh. That did it. She really was tired now, a state of delirious giggling about to set in. Never forgive himself? What a joke. The man had not a shred of conscience in his soul. Why not take advantage of him? It would serve him right. She could ride in his Jag and make him buy clothes and dinners for her, what the hell? He'd get nothing in return.

As she landed on the second-last step, her stomach wobbled again and stars formed in her field of vision. A tingling began somewhere deep in her chest and crept upward, both hot and cold sensations filling her. *I'm going to faint*, she realized. *No, not here. Not with him around!* She grabbed the banister and tucked her head down to stop it from happening,

Stephane's arms went around her waist, too tight for Zara's liking, but she hadn't much choice in the matter. *Oh, God.* Her body spoke to her. *Stop. Rest. Get strong. Someone needs you.*

"Hey, there," Stephane said, holding her close against him. "You're not well, are you? I should have seen that." He shook his head in admonition. "I'm taking you straight home."

Zara's vision cleared, and straightened her posture. What the hell did he mean? "This is home," she said weakly. "What are you talking about? Didn't you book me a hotel?"

"Are you okay to go on?" he asked. She nodded, and he began to move them both toward the exit. "No, I thought you deserved better. You'll see when we get there."

Once inside the Jag, Stephane pulled out a bottle of San Pellegrino from behind the passenger seat and handed it to

Zara. She knew she must look pale. She felt pale. Worse than pale, she felt like a ghost. She took the bottle from him and twisted it open, taking a swig of the refreshing liquid.

They drove north and, after a few turns onto treed boulevards and through swank communities, Stephane slowed in front of a stunning, Arthur Erickson-style creation that stood at the crest of a hill. Zara eyes panned its frontage, taking in the sleek, modern lines of stone and glass that formed a very impressive façade.

"Where are we?" Zara asked.

Stephane smiled. "You need a home, don't you? Temporarily anyway, so I thought I'd give you mine." Zara swiveled her head and fixed him with a look of utter disbelief. *Was the man crazy?* "Relax," he said in response to her withering stare. "I'm staying at the suites in my office building for now. The place is all yours." He parked the Jag and turned off the engine. "Look, I know you how feel about me, but I do care about you, Dolphin. I'm just trying to make you as comfortable as possible while we sort this mess out." He turned to look at her with his warm, hazel-eyed gaze. "Friends?"

Zara looked away, the sheer perfection of the mid-century residence drawing her full attention, mesmerizing her. She didn't remember Stephane owning this property. A week or so in his company seemed not a bad trade-off in exchange for losing herself inside this architectural thing of beauty.

"I wouldn't friend you on Facebook, Stephane. But in this case, I'll call a truce."

"Well, that's a start. The kitchen's all stocked up. Let's go in." He pulled the keys from the ignition and got out. As he moved to the passenger side, Zara opened her own door. She refused to act helpless in his presence. Before she could step out, he pulled the door all the way open and reached for her hand. With his big body blocking the way, her only way out was to take it. Resigned, she let him help her out of the Jag.

The home's interior was no less impressive than the outside. The open floor plan boasted gleaming walnut hardwood stretching from wall to wall. Fading daylight streamed from the multiple skylights spread across the room's steep-pitched roof line. Two cream-leather sofas flanked the room's main feature: a breathtaking, fieldstone fireplace.

Stephane aimed a remote at the hearth and, flames roared to life with the touch of a button. Zara stepped closer to it, the warmth drawing her in, begging her to sit before it. A plush area rug beckoned to her. She sank down on its soft surface in front of the fire and drew the cape around herself. She felt ready to sleep in the flames' radiant embrace. Her eyelids began to close.

The tinkle of plates and silverware jolted them open again. Stephane stood behind the counter of a galley kitchen on the far side of the room, pulling out dishes and utensils and reaching in and out of the stainless steel refrigerator. He'd removed his suit jacket, and Zara could see his broad chest and shoulders advertising themselves beneath the stylish silk dress shirt.

A burning sensation flowed to her cheeks. She blamed it on the fire, but knew better. The scene felt familiar, Stephane fussing in the kitchen while she watched. The Collingwood cottage. Oh yes, she'd tasted many of his dishes there, not all of them food. The man did love his food. Had he put on a little weight? Yes, she thought so.

Zara closed her eyes again. Nothing. Nothing would compare to a bowl of clam chowder right now. The memory of that first meal she and Dave had shared in his apartment seemed to fill her brain, blocking out everything else. The rich texture of it, how delicious it smelled, her recollection so vivid she swore she could taste it on her tongue. David. He'd done so much more than quelled her appetite. He fed her soul.

Her stomach growled and she felt desperately hungry, but not for food. She reached for the cellphone in her bag. Withdrawing it, she prayed for Dave's name to appear on its screen. Whether he'd fathered a child with another woman or not, didn't change the truth. She loved him.

Three missed calls. Mom. Mom. Mom. No surprise there. Tears began to sting her eyes. No word from him since she'd left Tenerife.

"Hey, don't fall asleep, I've got something special for you."

Zara put the phone away and looked up to see Stephane carrying a tray toward her. He set it down on a leather ottoman that served as a coffee table. Hesitating for a moment, he decided to fold his imposing frame and sit cross-legged on the floor next to her.

"Okay, picnic it is," he said, lifting a plate from the tray and offering it to her. She let the fur-trimmed cape slip from her shoulders as she took it from him. Under the circumstances she should have devoured every morsel. Red globe grapes, wedges of brie and cheddar, bruschetta piled high with olives and chunks of red onion. Thick slices of tomato layered with little orbs of bocconcini and drizzled in a balsamic glaze. A neat square of paté rounded out the display, nestled on a bed of arugula.

Zara stared at the artistic presentation in her lap. For the first time since she'd landed, she felt gratitude toward Stephane. "Merci." The word issued from her lips barely above a whisper. Somehow she couldn't find the will to eat anything.

He reached over and lifted a cheese wedge off the plate, and held it up to her mouth. "Come on, Dolphin, you need your strength."

Reluctantly, she opened her mouth and accepted his offering. The smooth texture of the brie mixed with the tart rind made a delicious pairing on her tongue. She chewed slowly, savoring it, and realized just how long it had been since she'd eaten. No wonder she'd nearly fainted in the stairwell.

But when she swallowed, her stomach had different ideas. It seemed to reject the rich little tidbit, and gave a sickening twist. Her face must have registered her discomfort, for Stephane quickly handed her a water goblet. She took a few swallows and set it back on the tray.

"I think I'm going to have to do this slowly," Zara said.

Stephane smiled a catlike grin and nodded. "Oui. Both of us."

Chapter Fourteen

This time the dolphin actually laughed. It spread its beak-ish jaws and cackled shrilly while bobbing its head up and down. Dave wanted to catch it, wrap his hands around its slippery throat and squeeze the life from it. Enough. Time to put an end to its relentless taunting. But it kept eluding him, each lunge he made for it causing it to move that much further out of reach.

It breached and dove, its tail smacking the surface of the water like a slap to his face. He dove along with it, determined to silence the obnoxious beast once and for all. Dave opened his eyes underwater, searching for it, but no luck. The trail of bubbles led him downward, down and down until his lungs felt like bursting.

Then he saw her.

Zara's nude body floated below him, suspended in mid-depth, neither rising nor sinking. Her long hair trailed upward with the current, her arms dangling adrift. He descended further, managing to reach her and put his arms around her. As he struggled to the surface, he stared into her open eyes, their green color paling in the underwater gloom.

Rising foot by foot, their ascent seemed to take forever. His lungs burned from lack of oxygen, felt himself starting to black out. He seemed unable to hold on to her, her body slipping from his grasp before he could reach the surface. Her limbs slid from his hands, the dark depths below sucking her downward just inches away from his goal. Dave's head broke the surface of the water and he inhaled precious air in massive gulps.

He awoke, gasping for breath as he opened his eyes and jerked his head off the flat surface it lay upon. Papers shifted position on the table and pencils rolled off its edge onto the floor. Jesus, he'd fallen asleep at his desk. Again.

And the dream had manifested itself, again.

Only now it took a darker, more ominous path. The feeling it left behind had somehow switched from helpless to hopeless. *The damned dolphin.* He wished he could crush it with his bare hands.

He rubbed his eyes as he straightened, the stiffness in his neck making him wince in pain. Cold sweat stuck the material of his shirt to his back. He blinked and glanced toward the windows, morning light streaming into the room. God, he couldn't keep going like this and still be sane by the time he got to Montreal. But the drawings wouldn't finish themselves. So he pushed on. They had to be ready for her when she came back. If she came back. No, he'd banished that kind of thinking from his mind. *When he brought her back.*

He'd been at it for nearly three days straight, the blueprints for La Dulce Zara. Based on sketches she'd found in her father's office, this villa would be the home that Zara wanted to build. On the site of El Mirador.

And Dave was determined to make it a reality.

He'd sent extra crews to clear the site, removing the fallen remains of the old building and shoring up the foundation. The tar sand field would be zoned off, and an interpretive center built around it, just like she'd wanted. The plans for that structure lay in Chico's workstation, having handed that part of the project over to the talented draftsman, who'd shown a creative flair for design that went quite beyond just running the CADD station and plotter.

The design for the villa Dave took on himself, wanting to see to every detail. He needed to show Zara that he'd invested his whole being into its design and construction, and more than that, invested his very heart and soul into their relationship, their future. Because he couldn't imagine it any other way.

He rose from his chair, tired muscles protesting after languishing behind his desk for God knew how many hours. His shirt wrinkled and sticky with sweat, and his jeans in need of a wash, he felt grimy beyond words and proceeded to peel the t-shirt off his body.

Two succinct knocks sounded outside his closed door, but the caller did not wait for a response. The girl entered the room at full speed, obviously expecting his office to be vacant since no one had seen him arrive.

Her name was Franca, an administrative assistant. She'd been pulling files on various topics for the project and held a stack of exactly that in one hand as she moved forward, looking at the papers and not where she was walking.

When she finally glanced up, she flinched at the sight of Dave's shirtless torso just a few feet ahead of her. A snowstorm of papers dropped to the carpet in her surprise.

"Oh, *lo siento,* Senor Parker," she stammered. "I didn't know you were here…ah…*perdoneme…*" She blushed furiously, but didn't seem able to look away. He watched her eyes move across his upper body and her face grow redder before she stooped to pick up the fallen documents. *"Por favor,"* she mumbled. "I didn't see you come in…"

Dave tossed the shirt over one shoulder, seeing no point in covering up.

"It's okay, Frankie," he said. "Nobody saw me come in. I just…never went home. Thanks for those files." He decided that more explanation wouldn't bring down the awkward meter a whole lot, so he just stood there, waiting, while she reconstructed her paper pile and placed it in his inbox.

She turned and hurried from the room, neglecting to close the door in her haste. She nearly bumped into Ernesto as he crossed the hallway toward the reception area. Her panicked movements made him look in the direction from which she'd come. Dave skulked about in his office at the end of the hall, zipping a jacket closed over his bare chest.

Ernesto made a beeline for him.

"What's going on in here?" Ernesto asked. "It's a good thing there aren't any clients in the office this morning."

Dave looked up, and ran his hand through his hair. "Oh. Sorry, Ern, ah…nothing." He stared blankly at Ernesto for a second. "I feel like shit," he announced. "I'm going to run home for a shower then I'll be back."

Ernesto worked his facial muscles for a moment then gave a single nod. "*Sí.* You look like shit, too." He cocked his head to one side. "Franca seemed rather high-energy though. Care to explain?"

Dave blinked and snapped out of his momentary hypnosis. He shoved his hands in his jacket pockets and gave a bewildered shake of his head. "What? I've been here all night. She came busting into my office without warning. I can't help what she saw, or what she's thinking," he said. "Or what you're thinking," he added. A tense silence hung in the air. "You know me better than that."

Ernesto smiled. "Of course I do. Franca on the other hand, does not. And I'm sure she'd like to. Keep it zipped, Youngblood." Dave raised his eyebrows and shot him a warning glance. Ernesto sobered. "And look after yourself.

You'll be no good to Zara, or any of us, if you work yourself to death."

Dave nodded and moved toward the door. "Message received. May I go now?"

Ernesto adjusted his stance and reached into his inside breast pocket. He withdrew a folded paper. *"Sí, puede.* All the way to Quebec," he said, flipping the flight itinerary toward him between his thumb and first knuckle.

Dave's shoulders relaxed as he exhaled. "Thanks, man," he said, taking the paper from him. "I'll be back. Got a few things to finish first."

*

He found the energy to take the stairs to his apartment two at a time. A quick shower and he'd be good as new. The thought of taking off for Montreal spurred him forward. The flight left tomorrow morning and a million things remained to do before then. He reached the third floor landing and pulled the key from his pocket. As he pushed it into the deadbolt, the door clicked open without the benefit of turning the key. Dave froze.

Had he been that out of it that he'd left his apartment unlocked since yesterday? He couldn't remember. He knew he needed sleep, but it wasn't like him to be that careless. Another possibility sprung to mind. An intruder had been, or still remained, inside. He pushed it open without a sound.

Nothing appeared out of place. No movement came from inside. Everything looked the same, smelled the same. He slipped further into the room. He checked the living area, the kitchen. Nothing unusual. Sadly, the dirty dishes hadn't washed themselves since he last looked. He walked noiselessly past the bathroom, to the bedroom, and did a double-take.

Curled comfortably asleep on his steel-frame bed, lay Ivette.

"Oh, for Christ's sake." The words escaped his lips in a tired groan, but loud enough to wake the sleeping beauty. Her head jerked away from where it had lain against her hands, folded prayer-like to one side. She turned her face toward him, and drew her arms slowly down to her sides. Her shapely body squirmed seductively on the bed's surface, her firm, tanned thighs visible through her high-slitted skirt.

He felt like someone had just rewound his life six months.

"What the fuck are you doing here? How—" Dave's voice broke off. He stared in stunned silence for a moment, his tired brain unable to react in any useful way. He ground his teeth at the sight of her, appearing completely comfortable in her languid pose upon his rumpled bed. What felt like a growl built in his throat. How dare she invade his private space. "How the hell did you get in here?"

In no hurry to get up, Ivette smoothed a lock of her thick, dark hair away from her face as she fixed her brown eyes on him. "Don't be angry, please. Don't you remember Samir? The caretaker?"

Dave shrugged, not caring who the hell Samir was. "No. Answer my question, dammit."

"Well," Ivette went on. "He remembered me. When I was more of a...regular visitor here." She cast him a coquettish smile. "He let me in."

So much for building security. He vaguely remembered the dark-complexioned caretaker. He would kick his Moroccan ass for this.

"Well, you can let yourself right back out, lady. You're not welcome here."

She twisted her body into a semi-upright position, leaning on one elbow. He watched her full breasts shift beneath her scoop-necked blouse as she did so, the pose accentuating her pronounced cleavage. No. He did not want to notice that. He wished she would disappear altogether. In fact, he should call the cops. She was trespassing after all. These thoughts lit up in his mind like elevator buttons, but he acted on none of them.

Her mouth seemed to tremble, her brown eyes glistened beneath what Dave thought must surely be crocodile tears.

"I never thought you to be this cruel, David," she said, her voice bordering on a whimper. "The mother of your child, unwelcome? You're not so heartless as that. I know you're not."

Her pleading voice made his head start to hurt. He pinched the bridge of his nose with a thumb and forefinger. Lack of sleep wasn't helping the situation.

"Stop saying that, I'm warning you." His words crawled out from between gritted teeth. "Save yourself a whole lot of trouble because I'll fight you on this. You've got no proof."

"Proof?" She began crying for real. "Do you think proof will change anything? Would it make you love me again?" She hid her face in her hands. "No. I can see that you hate me." Her sobs grew painful to hear. He wished she would stop. Resisting a crying female was difficult under the best of circumstances. Damn, he felt tired. He had no time for this.

"I don't hate you." The words came out on reflex without meaning attached to them. "But please stop this. You and I are not happening, ever. So stop with the lies, stop with the stalking," he said, his voice rising in angry desperation. "And tell me the goddamned truth! Why are you doing this?"

Startled, she dropped her hands and looked at him with fear in her eyes. "I'm pregnant. It's not a lie." Tears streaked shiny tracks down her cheeks. "I'm in trouble." She wiped at her face with the back of one hand. "You were so kind, before. I thought…you wouldn't abandon me. I thought you might be pleased." She snorted a lonely little laugh. "But I'm a fool. I can't afford to raise a child on my own. That's why I'm doing this."

Dave closed his eyes. *I can't deal with this. Not now.* "So it's money you're after?"

Ivette continued to dry her tears, sniffing. "If it has to come to that, if you want no part of me, or this child."

Dave exhaled, feeling like he might deflate with fatigue. He needed sleep. He needed to get back to the office. He didn't need this extra problem, but didn't see a quick way out if she wouldn't admit he wasn't the father. He hadn't time to argue. "Look. I have to be somewhere in a few hours. Please leave and we'll deal with this when I get back."

She gazed up at him, faint hope glimmering. "You'll help me?"

Dave shook his head, non-committal. "I'm not promising anything, Ivette. But I don't want to see you...suffer. I'm not that much of a bastard."

"I know. I've always known." She sat up and pushed herself off the bed. "You look so weary," she said, her voice softer than ever. She moved in close to him. "You should come to bed. Lie down, I'll see myself out." She reached out and touched his chest, her hands smoothing the material of his jacket. When he didn't move, she took hold of his arms and pulled him in the direction of the bed. A slight nudge, and he collapsed onto it.

It felt good to lie down. *Ernie told me to get some rest.* Couldn't think straight. He should get her out, lock the door behind her. *Shit.* His eyes felt so heavy, just keeping them open seemed too much of an effort.

He heard his front door slam shut, and he fell asleep without another thought.

Chapter Fifteen

"Yes, everything's under control, Mom," Zara said. "I'm staying with a friend until I get the insurance settled." She took a sip of her coffee as she held the phone to her ear. "I can have the furniture replaced, get some contractors working on the repairs, then I'll come back for awhile." Through the window of the little bistro Zara saw her friend approach the doors and waved to her.

"Sólo por un tiempo?" Marlena asked. "Then what? What shall I tell David? He's worried sick about you."

Zara frowned. "He's got enough to worry about." She watched the dark-haired girl enter the shop, and decided on one last thing to say. "When I come back, I want to sign over the El Mirador property to Jorge. Can you have Ernesto draw up the papers?"

Marlena's silence made Zara wince inwardly. "I'll speak to him about it, sweetheart. But I'm sure he'll want to wait until you return before doing anything."

"Okay, whatever you think. I've got to go, I'll call you again tonight, okay? Bye." She hung up, and the dark-haired girl squealed in delight as she trotted toward Zara, her arms wide for a hug. "Pammy!"

"Zara, Zara, Zaarah!" Parminder Singh threw her arms around her friend, her smile one of unconcealed joy.

Zara returned the hug. "Pam, it's so great to see you!" Both women giggled hysterically, then stepped back to get a good look at each other. "You look great, Pammy. Thanks for coming."

"Are you freaking kidding me, Z? We thought you'd fallen off the earth when you left…of course I came to see you! How is Spain? You've got a tan, you witch! Lots of time to lay on the beach, huh?" Pam's lips formed an 'o' and her chestnut eyes went wide. "Or, maybe a little *lay* on the beach, hey… hey?" She gave a backhand tap to Zara's sleeve and laughed at her own naughty joke.

Zara blushed a little, thinking how close to the truth her friend's words had landed. "Hey, I worked hard the last two months, wasn't all fun and games, you know," she replied in mock indignation.

Pam laughed, sweeping her sleek black bangs away from her face with one hand. Her teeth shone bright white in contrast to her cocoa-colored skin. "Okay, okay. So what's it like being the CEO of the company? I kept imagining you with your feet up on a big desk, smoking a cigar, or something. Is it fabulous?" She seated herself on a tall stool opposite Zara and began to peel off the scarf and plaid woollen coat she wore.

Zara snorted at Pam's vision of her. "It's hard work, is what! You can't imagine the number of decisions that need to be made in a day. The people are really great, though."

Pam ordered a latte. "That's awesome. I'm so happy for you, you must miss your dad though," she said. "How come you didn't work for the company here? Spain seems like a long way to go."

"Well," Zara shrugged. "He left me some property there, and I guess he thought I needed a break from cold winters."

She sighed and took another sip of coffee. "I'm not so sure I belong there."

Pam stirred her drink and regarded Zara with a friends' knowing gaze. "Z. Something's bothering you, c'mon. Out with it. You jet off to Spain, take over the family business, inherit property, now you're back looking glum as a lost dog. What's up?"

Zara swallowed the last of her coffee. In that moment, she realized she probably shouldn't even be drinking coffee, if what she suspected were true. She needed to confide in somebody, and she trusted Parminder, her old roommate from university. Though they'd chosen very different career paths, Pam a nurse, and Zara an architect, they'd remained best friends.

"I got a call." She looked Pam in the eyes. "My condo's been trashed."

Pam's dark eyes went wide with concern.

"And my car stolen." Zara went on.

"No…not the Beamer…" Pam gasped.

Zara nodded. "My place is ruined, but insurance will take care of that. My car, not so sure. It's still missing."

"Oh, Z, I'm so sorry. What are you going to do? Where are you staying? Why didn't you call me earlier and come stay with me?"

Zara smiled and reached out to touch Pam's arm, glad she had such a friend. "Thanks, Pammy. But it's all arranged. All I have to do is sign a few papers, and go shopping for new stuff. How bad can that be, huh?"

Pam returned her smile, but didn't stop there. "You didn't answer my question."

Zara waved it off. "It doesn't matter. I…have something else I need to ask you." Pam tilted her brown-skinned face toward her in curiosity. Zara took a deep breath. "Do you have the number for that doctor you used to work for, Dr. Klein?"

Pam looked at her steadily. "The obstetrician?" Zara nodded. "I think so. What are you saying, Z?"

"You know what I'm saying. I need to make sure."

Pam scrambled for her cell phone in her purse. "I'll text it to you. Oh, Z, what's going on? Please tell me."

Zara looked away, out the front windows of the shop, and felt the familiar sting of tears start to build. "I can't tell you the whole story, yet. But I will, as soon as I know."

The silver Jaguar pulled up at the curb outside the bistro. "I've got to go, but promise you won't breathe a word to anybody. Please?"

Pam's eyes followed Zara's glance. She felt sure Pam recognized the vehicle. "Oh, Z, you have to be joking. Not that shit-head lawyer."

"Good God, no. It's not what it looks like, Pam, I…" Zara's words trailed off. She motioned to her with her thumb and pinky extended as she moved toward the exit. *"I'll call you."*

Stephane bounded to the curb to open the Jaguar's door for her, his blond hair shining in the morning sunlight. The temperature had dropped overnight, and a pebbled shell of ice covered the sidewalk. He clutched Zara's elbow as he guided her into the passenger seat. As she watched him return to his place behind the wheel, she noticed he'd exchanged his standard two-piece suit for a plain black turtleneck and wool blazer. His wardrobe choice made his shoulders appear even broader than usual, and a pair of Diesel jeans fitted snugly over his powerful thighs. A big man, any way she looked at him.

He swung into the driver's seat and a waft of Hugo Boss mingled with the crisp outdoor air as he closed the door. "Did you sleep well?" he asked. "I have the insurance documents at my office. After we take care of those, how does shopping grab you?" He smiled in something approaching delight, looking like a kid skipping school to head for the mall.

"For furniture," Zara said stiffly. She found his enthusiasm unsettling. This wasn't a damn field trip. She just wanted to get her place fixed up and be done with it.

"And? C'mon, Dolphin, you have no warm clothes to wear. Let me treat you to a few other things."

"I have things, at the condo, if you'll let me get them. You can drop the sugar daddy act, anytime."

His expression bordered on hurt. "That's uncalled for. I'm just trying to be nice. Have it your way." He started the ignition, but remained in park. "Speaking of Daddy," he continued. "There's something else I need to discuss with you."

Zara eyed him warily. "And what might that be?"

"Your office here. Flynn Enterprises, I mean. I'm afraid it's not doing very well."

Her comfort level dropped several notches. What the hell would he know about Flynn Enterprises? "What do you mean?"

"There's been a big staff turnover. The RFPs have dropped off severely. There's no work for those who are left. It needs a change in management, the board structure. It may be in danger of shutting down."

Zara stared at him, incredulous. How did he know things about the company that she didn't? "How do you know this, Stephane? It's news to me, and I'm the CEO. Explain."

Stephane leaned back, the charcoal-grey leather of the headrest giving a characteristic squeak while releasing its musky scent. The air inside the vehicle seemed filled with masculine intent. He turned his face toward her, and pushed up his mirror-lensed Vuarnet shades with one finger.

"I'm a businessman, sweetie. I read the stock reports. It's not exactly insider knowledge. Besides, it concerns you. I follow everything that concerns you. Is that so much of a shock?"

"Am I supposed to be flattered? I'm way past that, Stephane. I don't succumb to your attentions anymore. You're snooping. Why?"

Stephane shook his head in exasperation. "Snooping," he scoffed. "Public knowledge is not snooping. But if you think I have a personal interest in the affairs of your company, you're right. As for why, I should think that would be obvious. We were a couple once, Zara. I want to see you do well. Why do you think I'm handling these insurance issues? I could have had any number of agents contact you, but I didn't. I chose to look after you personally. Doesn't that tell you something? I believe in you, despite your feelings for me. Or lack thereof." He leaned in a little closer. "I'd like to change that, if you'll let me."

Zara worked her tongue inside her mouth, not believing him for a second. She'd been taken in by his flattery before. As for the company, she needed to see this for herself. "Far too late for that, Stephane. Go cast your spell on someone else. When we're done with the insurance stuff, take me to the Flynn office. You can start by proving you're not the liar I remember."

*

"He's not answering his phone," Ernesto said, disconnecting the call and stuffing his smartphone into his chest pocket. "But, I suspect he's taken my advice and is trying to get some rest."

"When does his flight leave?" Marlena asked.

"Seven a.m. tomorrow. Does she know he's coming?"

Marlena shook her head. "I almost told her, but I know my daughter. She wants to do everything herself. She said she wants to sign over El Mirador to Jorge."

Ernesto sighed and looked out over the water. Sunset cast luminous threads of gold and rose across its choppy surface. "She is…*muy independiente. Como su madre.*"

Marlena gave him a sharp glare then laughed. "No, Ernesto. I've never been independent. Not like Zara." She began to pick up the remains of their dinner. They sat on a park bench along the waterfront, take-out containers and napkins spread between them. "But you know, I guess I never had to be. I had my family, then I had Tristan."

Ernesto stood and tossed the rubbish into a nearby bin. Marlena drew her pashmina tighter about her shoulders against the December breeze. He turned to face her and held out his hand.

"And you had me," he said, his voice tinged with regret. "You didn't seem to notice."

She met his gaze with honest eyes. A look so free of guile or deceit it made his heart ache. A truer, more genuine person he could not imagine in all the world. She would speak the truth, and he hoped it would be what he desperately wanted to hear.

She slipped her hand silently into his. "I noticed. *Soy afortunada.* I am lucky."

They remained that way for several seconds, he standing and she seated on the bench. All the years putting aside his feelings, forcing them out of his memory just to function and get on with his life, seemed to boil up in his chest and drive his next action like a locomotive. He pulled her, almost harshly, off the bench and into his arms. Her slim body landed against his chest and he held her there, firm and in control. He would not miss his chance again.

His hand slipped under her chin, fitting it into the V between his thumb and fingers and tilting her face toward him. "Marly," he said, his voice low and needful. "Don't let luck slip away. Be with me now." Her brown eyes widened. He felt he could see straight in to her soul, and yes, a flicker of desire dwelt deep within.

He kissed her, his decades of longing converging in that moment. A moment of passion, of hope, and of promise. Her lips melted soft and moist against his without hesitation or resistance. *Thank the moon and stars*, he thought. She was kissing him back.

Chapter Sixteen

Yes. That felt good. His dick hardened with each gentle stroke of her hand, arousing him. His mind floated toward consciousness, stringing bits of reality together like a jigsaw puzzle forming a finished scene. *It's all been a bad dream.* Zara lay here with him, urging him to wakefulness and carnal pleasures, just as it should be. Her warm lips nuzzled the back of his neck and graced it with tiny kisses.

Dave inhaled in slow satisfaction, a smile playing at the corners of his mouth. The jigsaw puzzle began to fracture and fall away piece by piece. His eyes snapped open in alarm. *Not real. I'm alone in my apartment, Zara is thousands of miles away...Oh, God.*

He didn't know how long he'd been asleep. The bedroom lay dark, but the warm presence snuggled against his back assured him he was definitely not alone.

And someone's hand was on his cock.

He jerked away, nearly falling off the edge of his bed. What the hell time was it? Christ, he had a plane to catch! He pushed himself apart from the body lying next to him and rolled away, dropping to his knees on the floor. He scrambled for the lamp on the night table. He switched it on, the sudden brightness making him blink and squint in the direction of the bed. *Holy Christ, I thought she'd left.*

Ivette's long, smooth body lay on her side, her dark eyes moist and beckoning. She wore next to nothing, a lacy pushup bra and matching thong in a color he couldn't begin to describe. She was a damn sexy sight, and his dick agreed. If this were another time, another place, he knew his next move would have been something less than gentlemanly.

"I told you to get out. What the hell do you think you're doing?" he asked, his voice loud but still rough with sleep. He glanced down to discover his fly wide open, with his cock exposed and inconveniently alert.

She didn't move, save for the tantalizing rise and fall of her breasts as she breathed. "I tried. I meant to leave," she whispered. "But I couldn't. I wanted…our baby to be with his father, even for this little while."

This had gone too far. He felt like strangling her and fucking her at the same time. Enough. He had to get out of here. He spotted his cell phone on the nightstand and grabbed for it. She'd turned it off, damn her. When the screen came to life, it read 5:10 a.m. Message notifications began buzzing in steady succession.

"Shit!" he yelled aloud. "Get dressed. I don't care what you thought, or what you wanted. Just get out!"

He made the bathroom in two lunging steps and slammed the door. He'd barely make it to the airport now, never mind finishing the drawings at the office. Taxis were unreliable at best, and there was no time to lose. He punched one of the missed numbers on his cell, of the only person that could help him now.

*

Alain Labelle leaned against a lamppost on Rue Peel, sizing up the building before him. Its plain brick front sported no balconies or fire escapes, its security system nothing special; easily bypassed. The inside he'd already studied during his meeting with Vanier. Business hours ended at four p.m. and as he peered through the dusk, no night patrols seemed to be engaged. *Morceau de gateau,* he mused. A piece of cake.

His cell phone vibrated in the pocket of his baggy overcoat. He reached for the device while still staring at the building frontage. When he diverted his gaze to its screen, he considered it for a moment before punching the button.

"Necesito su ayuda, mi amigo," came a rasping voice.

Alain clucked his tongue in response. *Well, well. So the Spaniard needed help, did he.* *"¿Es la verdad? Por que?"*

"Your Spanish es terriblé, ami."

Alain shrugged. *"Si,* and your French sucks. Anglais then, eh? What you want, spic?"

A dangerous silence followed. "Watch your big mouth, frog. Your English isn't much better. I need a place to disappear for a while."

"For how long? The safe house, she is…*occupado.*"

The voice grew rougher. "A few weeks. Maybe a month. Get rid of whoever's in there."

"Oh, I no can do that, ami." Alain played coy on purpose. He hated the Spaniard for a deal gone wrong a few years back, resulting in the death of a friend by drug overdose. Alain avoided jail only by sheer luck that time, and for some unfathomable reason, the Spaniard kept in touch.

"You'd better start thinking you can, friend. If you know what's good for you. I'm in town, so empty it, quick."

Alain glanced again at the brick building. "Perhaps another place, eh? Give me some time."

"Make it fast, frog. I'll be waiting." The line dropped.

Alain slipped the phone back into his pocket. An unexpected turn of events. The bigshot wanted the little Frenchman's help. Now here was an opportunity too good to miss. He just might need a temporary partner. Glancing at the building once more, he nodded in agreement with himself. A partner in crime.

Alain loped away from his spot where Rue Peel and Boulevard Rene Levesque intersected. He had some business yet to attend to and, after a walking a few blocks, fished a key from his coat pocket.

The BMW sat where he'd parked it in an alley, the engine still warm. It had been a pleasure to retrieve it from the storage locker where it had hidden for the past week. He'd liked to have driven it around for awhile after stealing it from the Westmount neighborhood, but Vanier said no. He wanted it taken to the outskirts of the city tonight and dumped, so that's where it would go. *But he never said exactly when.* He got in and turned on the ignition. A nice night for a joyride.

*

Zara stood in the middle of her bedroom, making what order she could from the mass of clothes, bedding and furniture that lay strewn from wall to wall. At least she could salvage some of her wardrobe. Although Stephane had been correct about her needing warm clothes, she refused to take any more charity from him. The fur cape had been bad enough, and she'd only worn it because of the snow. She had no intention of ever touching it again.

Glad to be alone after a long, depressing day, she had time to think while picking out some sweaters, jeans and shoes. After filing the insurance claim, they'd visited several furniture stores and ordered the needed replacements. Stephane had already booked contractors for the cleanup and repairs, but they wouldn't be here for a few days. This gave her time to go through things.

By far the worst part of the day came after lunch. A visit to the Montreal office of Flynn Enterprises added yet another layer of problems Zara didn't need. She hadn't realized how much the current economic situation had affected the North-

Am operations, and she felt a twinge of embarrassment that Monsieur know-it-all Vanier had this information before she did.

They were unable to meet with Rejean Houle, the ops manager, when they arrived. A technician informed them he'd been called to a meeting with the only major client contract they had left, one they couldn't afford to lose. Rejean himself had only taken the ops position recently, after several senior staff had left to pursue other opportunities, leaving him, a relatively inexperienced project manager, in charge.

Several seats on the board of directors were vacant as well. Strategic direction was imperative, but Zara knew that she herself was in no position to provide it. For more reasons than one.

However, the more they discussed the situation, Zara became grudgingly aware of one person who could. As much as she hated the idea, Stephane Vanier could very well fit the role of Board President of Flynn Enterprises. Smart, successful and connected, Stephane had undeniable business sense, and killer instincts to match. The thought of him taking a piece of her company the same way he'd taken a piece of her heart made her want to puke.

The condo seemed cold, and too quiet all of a sudden. She shoved aside some of the mess to find her iPod dock and speakers that used to sit on her nightstand. Somehow it had escaped the thief's notice and she plugged it in, connected the iPod and set it to shuffle.

It seemed ages since she'd listened to music, and remembered with sadness the sounds of Dave's guitar as he'd played for her what seemed like so long ago. What was he doing now? Mending his relationship with the she-goddess, accepting his responsibility as a father? The mental picture sent a stab of pain through her very soul. She loved him in spite of all of it. What they'd had together couldn't have been wrong. There had to be some mistake.

She would see Dr. Klein tomorrow, but she couldn't let Stephane know this, and needed a way to get to her appointment. As she debated what to do, she tried to gain some calm and let the music infuse her. The lyrics drifted to her ears.

> *There she was just a girl,*
> *She expected the world.*
> *But it flew away from her reach,*
> *So she ran away in her sleep.*
> *And dreamed of paradise...*

She closed her eyes and let the tears flow uninterrupted.

Chapter Seventeen

"Ernie?" His voice sounded strained and desperate. "Sorry I missed your calls. I fell asleep. I hate to have to ask you this, but can you get me to the airport?"

Ernesto inhaled and shifted position to talk more clearly into his cell phone. "Of course, David. I've been trying to reach you. I'll be right there." He disconnected and set the phone down. He gently pulled his other arm out from beneath Marlena's shoulders as the two of them lay intertwined on the couch. She stirred, and her eyes fluttered open.

"What's going on?" she murmured.

Ernesto had waited for this moment for so long, he felt reluctant to move. He and Marlena had driven to Ernesto's modest, but comfortable, house on the outskirts of Malaga after their dinner on the waterfront. They'd spent the evening watching TV and sharing a fine bottle of Sangiovese. A perfect ending to a perfect day, as if they'd been together all those missing years. Though he knew better than to believe it could become anything serious. She was still in love with her late husband.

"It's David. He overslept. I need to get him to the airport," Ernesto whispered, planting a gentle kiss on her cheek. He rubbed her arm up and down in a reassuring caress. "Wait for me here?"

Marlena brushed a hand across her forehead, pushing a lock of hair aside. "I'll wait," she said. "What time is it?"

Ernesto sat forward, slipping on his watch that he'd left on the coffee table. "Five fifteen. I've got to hurry."

"Adelante. Don't let him miss that flight." Marlena straightened also, leaning her chin on his shoulder and rubbing his back. "Tell him *Vaya con Dios."*

Ernesto smiled, and wished he could remain here in the dark with her. The early hours of morning always brought him a feeling of suspended solitude, where time stood still and the pressures of his workaday life seemed miles away. *"Sí, lo haré."* He slipped an arm around her waist and squeezed. "Just be here when I get back."

With difficulty, he pulled himself from her embrace and headed for the door.

*

The December evening held little light save for the street lamps. Parminder hoisted her duffel bag over her shoulder as she left the gym and stepped out onto the darkened street. At the end of her long day, she could not get her visit with Zara out of her mind. She worried that her friend was in trouble, and keeping secrets from her. She'd seemed very stressed, untalkative, and apparently keeping company again with the douchebag lawyer that had broken her heart once already. Worse, the suggestion that Zara might be pregnant made Pam heartsick for her dearest college buddy.

She breathed in the chill night air, and exhaled in a frosty cloud. Her muscles felt tired, but good after her workout. She felt the urge for a cigarette, but forced it to the back of her mind. No sense ruining the benefits of a good workout on a habit she'd worked hard to break. *Health professionals should set an example*, she thought, and as a nurse, she refused to be seen smoking. She trudged down the block toward the bus stop across the street. A little farther from home than she would have preferred, the inexpensive rates of this gym on the outskirts of town made up for it. An extra bus ride wasn't that big a deal.

She came to the corner and pushed the walk button. Waiting under a street lamp, she wondered if she actually still had any cigarettes in her purse, and decided to take a look while standing in the light. She unzipped her handbag and reached in. The walk light chirped its birdlike signal, and Parminder stepped one foot onto the pavement.

A sudden whine came from her left and a fast-moving vehicle sped around the corner. It headed straight for her, its headlights off. Parminder stopped, paralysed in mid-stride as the car screeched to a halt, missing her by scarcely a meter. She retreated to the sidewalk and stared wild-eyed at the driver.

A man, his own eyes staring back in equal horror to hers, leaned forward against the wheel in response to his pounding on the brakes. Through the windshield, she could see his scruffy beard and unruly shock of dark hair that stuck out to one side. She could feel her heart beating fiercely, puffs of steaming breath escaping her lips in rapid bursts. Neither of them moved for a frozen minute, then the driver seemed to regain his wits and hit the gas.

Parminder swung her gym bag at the offending vehicle, and it grazed the rear panel with a harmless thud as it moved swiftly out of range. *Maniac,* she thought angrily, and took a good look at the car to make a mental note of the license plate.

With a shock, Pam realized she knew that plate number. And more--she knew that car. A champagne-gold BMW that belonged to her best friend, Zara Flynn.

*

When Stephane arrived at the condo, Zara's eyes felt like a pair of boiled onions from crying. She'd filled two shopping bags worth of her belongings, and he stooped to collect them as she took a last look around the place.

"Dolphin?" he asked quietly. "Are you okay?"

For such a heartless bastard, he put on a pretty good act of concern, but she wasn't buying it. She trained her red-rimmed eyes on him. "What do you think? Would you be okay in my situation?" She waved her arm across the dishevelled room then pulled a wad of Kleenex from her purse to blow her nose. "You're such an asshole."

Stephane stayed silent for a moment then shrugged. "If it makes you feel better, I'm willing to be called an asshole. I can take it."

Having no place to toss out the tissue, she stuffed it in her coat pocket. Noticing that he made no further comment, she eyed him curiously. He actually seemed at a loss as to what to say, and suddenly wished she could take her words back. Being confrontational would solve nothing.

"I'm sorry." The words slipped out of her mouth before she realized it. They stood there staring at each other, until Zara broke eye contact. "Let's get out of here."

"Sure," he said, and they made their way outside with her packages in tow. They drove to his house in silence.

When they pulled into the driveway, Zara spoke. "I need a car for tomorrow."

"Oh? You don't like the way I drive?"

She shook her head. "No, that's not it. I have some things I'd like to do…alone." She looked away from him as he put the Jag in park. "And, you have work. You've already missed a day, and I don't need a babysitter."

"I know that. But I don't mind, really."

In her peripheral vision, she caught his shy smile. It reminded her of Dave, and a ripple of pain shuddered through her. "It's not necessary. Can you get me a rental?"

He elbowed the driver's door open, his smile widening. "I can do better than that. C'mon."

Unsure what he meant by that, Zara got out and followed him into the house. Setting her bags down, he crossed the foyer and reached into the shallow drawer of a console table that stood against one wall. He tossed something into the air toward her and Zara caught it with one hand. A set of keys jingled in her palm and she shot him a questioning glance.

He gestured toward the connecting door to his garage, and opened it. She peered in, and saw a familiar sight. The little red MG they'd driven on some of their weekend trips to Collingwood, sat parked inside. Damn, she'd loved that car. And he'd let her have it, carte blanche? Huh. The guy presented one surprise after another, and Zara didn't like it. Or the smug look on his face. *He must be up to something.*

"Does it have gas?' she asked.

Stephane laughed. "Jesus, you really don't trust me, do you? Yes, it has gas."

Zara stepped back, her arms folded in front of her chest. "Okay then, I'll take it."

He shut the door and stood facing her, his jaw dropping a little. He gave his head a slight shake and took a step toward her. "What do I have to do to make you trust me?" he said, his voice slipping into the bedroom version she remembered very well.

Zara stood her ground. He moved closer still.

"I know I hurt you." His eyes searched hers with an honesty that Zara didn't expect. "And that's the biggest regret of my life right now." He reached out the short distance between them and took her by the shoulders. "I really am an asshole. To lose your trust, and let you get away."

His nearness made her both uneasy and a little dizzy. Maybe it was Hugo Boss, or perhaps some weird pheromone he was giving off. Either way, she felt hypnotized, like prey frozen in the sights of a deadly snake. "I trusted you once. Didn't turn out so well," she replied, her voice cracking. "And once an asshole, always an—"

"I can change," he interrupted. "I want to change," he whispered, so close now his lips hovered mere inches away from hers. "I'd do anything for you." His hands moved up to frame her ears, his hazel gaze so intense it made Zara afraid. "I want you…"

As he moved to kiss her, anger broke the spell and she thrust her hands between them, pushing forcibly against his chest.

"Life's full of disappointments, isn't it?" She shoved him away with all her might. "Have you checked your watch? Your nine o'clock girlfriend must be waiting."

He looked stunned, as if resistance was something new to him. He opened his mouth to speak when his iPhone went off in his jacket pocket. With relief, Zara watched him break eye contact and reach for the phone. He glanced at the screen and tilted his head back, his expression changing from one of annoyance, to astonishment. He thumbed the screen and answered it.

"Oui, c'est Vanier," he said curtly. He turned away, as though the conversation wasn't meant for Zara's ears. "Oui." A pause. "Non! "Où est-ce ?" Another pause. "Sérieusement?' He turned back to Zara with a smile of incredulousness. "C'est fantastique. Oui, merci." He lowered the phone and looked straight at her.

"It's the police. They've found your car."

*

Having completed his task with the BMW, Alain disconnected the call. Vanier certainly had an acting career to fall back on, he thought. And he might need one, too, once this little venture blew up in Vanier's face. The conversation sounded convincing. He assumed that the young lady had been in the same room, and listening. He stood outside the rear entrance to the brick building on Rue Peel, waiting. When another man approached, he moved under the overhang and bypassed the security code with ease. The man, wearing a black jacket, followed him and they both passed over the threshold. Once inside, they moved together down a darkened hallway to a service elevator.

"You're sure it's safe," the man commented.

"Oui, safe as one can be when hiding from the law. What have you done this time, Spic? Alain yanked open the safety gates.

"None of your business, frog. I'll be gone in a week or two, and it will be as if I was never here, *comprender?*" the man said, with sinister emphasis on the last word.

Alain sniggered. "You should be nice to me, amigo. Remember, you help me, and I help you. That simple. Tell me why you here."

Carlos gave him a cold stare. "Some stash found its way to the *polizia* in Cadiz. It mustn't be connected to me, see? As soon as someone takes the fall for it, I can go back." He took a step toward Alain as the lift platform clattered to a stop. "And I intend to go back."

Alain shrugged. "I hope you do, for both our sakes."

"I didn't want to leave. I had no choice. I have a good thing going in Malaga. I just hope she's still there when I return."

"She?" Alain asked with sarcasm in his voice. "Elle?" he repeated in French. His manner turned comedic as he snorted a curt laugh. "*Elle* has been the undoing of many a man such as you. You're better off without *elle*, mon ami."

"What do you know," Carlos sneered as he stepped off the platform. "You've probably not had any real pussy in your whole miserable life."

Alain followed after closing the safety gate and sending the platform back to the main floor. "I know I won't ever be compromised by a piece of ass. Can't say the same for you, eh?" He led his visitor to another door with a keypad. He entered his stolen code and the light glowed green. He pulled the latch open and peered through the crack. He pressed his finger to his lips and drew the opening wider.

They stepped in to what resembled a hotel suite with a table and two chairs, a mini-kitchen and a queen-sized bed. "I hope you no have luggage," Alain said. "Don't want the place to look lived-in."

Carlos tossed a pack of cigarillos on the table. "Just these," he said. "Got a light?"

Alain clucked his tongue. *"No fumar, estupid!* Maybe you just wanna walk to the police station down the street and save time."

Flipping up his collar, Carlos hunkered down into the warmth of his jacket. "Fucking cold here. Need something to keep warm."

"Don't worry," Alain said. "I hear it's plenty warm in hell. You'll be there soon, unless you play nice."

Carlos scowled. "What do you want me to do?"

"See this wall?" Alain pointed. "On the other side are some very pretty things. And you're going to help me steal them."

*

The white-haired head moved through the crowd, edging to the front of the group that waited for the arriving passengers. Dave recognized the familiar loping gait as the older man stepped into view. Having nothing more than a backpack for luggage, Dave slung it firmly over one shoulder and walked toward him.

Bruce Parker smiled at the sight of him and stood still as Dave approached. The old man watched him with the look of an artist admiring his own work. In a way, Dave supposed, it was the truth. "Hey, Dad. Good of you to come all this way."

Bruce put his arm around his son's shoulders. A few inches shorter, Bruce had to reach up a bit to make the gesture. "No problem, bud. How was your flight?"

Dave yawned. "Long and uncomfortable, actually. But I'm here. How's Mom?"

Bruce gave him a few swats on the back before releasing Dave from his hold. "Fine, fine. She's sorry to have missed you, but she's out in the Okanagan with your sister for the holidays. I'm going out there myself the week before Christmas. You look great, son. Tired, but great. C'mon, I've brought something for you." He pointed to the exits and began moving them forward.

"Brought something? Like what? You've already gone out of your way just to meet me here."

"No, no, a stroke of luck, really. I was coming up for an auction in Drummondville this weekend anyway. No sweat."

They walked to the parking garage and Dave's eyes brightened as he spotted the familiar vehicle. His '03 Mustang sat between two concrete columns, its slick paint job and chrome detail shining even in the dim light.

Dave smiled. "You've been looking after her, I see." To say that Bruce Parker was a bit of a car nut would be an understatement. A mechanic for most of his working career, he'd been fixing, buying, selling and tinkering with cars for as long as Dave could remember. The Mustang appeared in top condition thanks to Bruce's tender care. "Hey, you weren't planning to auction her off, were you?" Dave asked, mock suspicion in his voice.

Bruce laughed. "Don't give me any ideas. Drive it away before I change my mind."

Dave looked at his father with a newfound admiration. "Thanks." It dawned on him all the things fatherhood meant. He'd do well to be half the dad Bruce had been. *Someday,* he thought resolutely. "How are you getting back to Drummondville?"

Bruce shrugged. "I've got a buddy meeting me downtown who's headed for the auction too. Thought we'd grab a bite to eat, then you can drop me off with him."

Dave nodded. "Okay. And how are you getting back to Thunder Bay?"

"It's an auction, Dave," he deadpanned. "When have you known me not to come away with at least one set of wheels at an auction?"

At that moment, Dave realized he'd come by his comedic tendencies honestly. He mirrored his Dad's sense of humor perfectly. With a chuckle and a vague notion about an apple and a tree, he strode over to the Mustang's driver side. "Right. Where to, then?"

Bruce moved to the passenger side. "Where else? Schwarz Deli."

With a grin, Dave tossed his backpack in the rear seat and slid behind the wheel. She felt, and smelled, as good as he remembered, with her hip-hugging bucket seat and soft-grip stick shift. The familiar scent of leather and patchouli pervaded the cabin; a man's space. Bruce handed him the keys, and the Mustang roared to life.

"So, tell me about this girl that's brought you all the way back across an ocean," Bruce said.

Dave sighed. He threw the stick into gear and told his father everything.

Chapter Eighteen

Zara awoke in the white-walled bedroom of Stephane's house with a headache. In addition to the intermittent bouts of nausea, headaches seemed to be plaguing her lately. Another symptom, or just stress? *Yeah. Stress. I'm going with stress.*

Despite this, she managed to smile, remembering the good news from the night before. Her BMW had been found in an industrial area of the city, apparently unscathed; as if someone had simply borrowed it for an errand. Stephane said the police were towing it to the local impound and they could pick it up later today. A bright spot in an otherwise painful trip.

But until then, she'd have to drive the little MG to her appointment. She hoped she remembered how to drive a stick. It had been awhile. Nursing the pain behind her eyes, she sat up in bed, deciding whether to have a shower or a nice warm bath to ease the headache and get ready for the day.

As she glanced around the room, a stray thought wandered into her head. What would it be like to wake up in this room every day? Beautiful in its simplicity and elegance, the walls sported a subtle tone-on-tone paint finish. Exposed dark timbers accentuated the high ceiling. The carved-wood sleigh bed she'd slept in offered exquisite luxury, piled high with a down comforter and plump, heaven-soft pillows. A spectacular chandelier hung above the bed, a unique, swirling tempest of metal branches studded with almond-shaped bulbs. When lit, it resembled a galaxy of stars descending into the room.

My brain must be going soft. The undeniable charm, looks and taste of the womanizing Stephane Vanier were beginning to work their magic upon her once again.

No. She would not allow that. She clambered from the dreamy bed and padded across the plush carpet to the ensuite. She flicked the light switch, and the gold-veined marble of the tub enclosure and double vanity gleamed in the soft light of the wall sconces. Again, she could not deny the man had taste.

She filled the tub and checked the medicine cabinet for Tylenol. Nada. The vanity drawers yielded none either, so she donned a short robe that she'd brought from the condo, and went to try her luck the kitchen. Reaching the end of the hall that connected to the main living area, Zara stopped short.

Fussing with the coffee machine, and wearing nothing but a pair of workout pants, stood Stephane. *What the hell? Had he spent the night? The rat!* He'd promised to stay at his downtown suite. She made a scoffing noise. When could she ever believe a word this snake-in-the-grass said?

He turned to look in her direction at the sound. His eyes raked her up and down. Zara clutched the thin robe tighter around herself, knowing it didn't hide much. She found her voice before he did. "I heard you leave last night. What are you doing here?"

Stephane stopped fiddling with the machine, but continued to stare at her. A smile began twitching at the corners of his mouth. "I did leave. Then I remembered some papers I needed from my home office, and came back. I ended up reading through them for hours and, well. Forgive me. I just crashed in the den."

Her eyes narrowed as she listened to his plausible, yet underhanded story.

"I'll make you coffee–" he offered.

"I can't drink coffee." She cursed silently at her verbal slip. "I have a headache, and coffee makes it worse," she said, to add some credibility to the statement. "Do you have any Tylenol?"

"Yeah, sure," he said lightly, as if grateful she'd changed the subject. He turned and opened a cabinet next to the fridge. Facing away, his brawny shoulders were in full view, the curve of his spine creating a pleasant line down his back. Looking past him, Zara could see a quite a collection of bottles within, vitamins and protein supplements and more. From among them he produced a familiar red-lidded container and tapped a few e-Z tabs into his hand.

Zara stood in place at the edge of the hallway, not moving. "And some water," she said. From the fridge he grabbed a bottle of Evian and brought both the water and the medicine over to where she stood. "Thanks," she said, taking it from him. "Now if you wouldn't mind, could you go sleep somewhere else, like you promised?"

She found herself looking directly at his naked chest to avoid eye contact. He may have bulked up a bit since she'd seen him last, but his powerful musculature remained undiminished, and difficult to ignore. Dark chest hair feathered out across his pectorals, and continued in a line down the middle of his torso, ending just above his navel. Yikes. His navel. Her private muscles convulsed in an unbidden reaction. She started to back away when he suddenly reached out and caught hold of the silver dolphin that still hung round her neck.

"Hey, I remember this," he said. "I didn't know you still wore it." He fingered it for a moment then closed his hand around it. He tipped her chin upward with his other hand. "That tells me something."

She had no choice but to look into those hazel eyes, and listen to the dangerously soft and sexy voice. Warning bells rang in Zara's head, bringing the already present pain to a fever pitch. *Why did I wear this stupid thing? I meant to take it off so many times...* She jerked away and the chain broke, leaving Stephane clutching the pendant in his fist, the silver strands dangling in the air.

"Hey," he called, as she turned and bolted for the bathroom. His footsteps lagged behind her only a pace or two, as she raced down the hall. Too late. Stephane closed the distance easily, catching hold of her and sandwiching her with his heavy body against he bathroom door.

His breath blew warm across her shoulders as he spoke. "What's wrong, babe? Talk to me...I'm not the enemy. Please let me help you."

"Let me go," she begged. "I don't feel well...please." Zara could feel his chest moving in and out, as well as the rest of his bumps and bulges pressing in tight against her back. She didn't stand a chance if he decided to use brute force. He took a few more deep breaths, and when she felt a momentary relax of his muscles, lunged forward into the bathroom, slamming and locking the door behind her.

She heard his fist thumping against it. She clapped the red tablets onto her tongue and gulped down the water. "Leave me alone," she called out.

His voice bordered on desperation. "Zara, I don't understand. I've said I'm sorry, I hate myself for having hurt you. I've loved taking care of you these past few days. I love seeing you in my house. I...I've pictured it a thousand times since you left. You have no idea."

As she pulled off her robe and stepped into the tub, it occurred to her it wasn't the only hot water she'd be getting into. Zara shivered even while surrounded by the warm water. It struck her with alarming certainty that Stephane had planned this from the beginning. He wanted her back. He practically held her captive. And she'd let it happen.

Her head felt near exploding with pain. "Fuck off," she yelled. "I have stuff to do. Just go get my car back, and after that, I'm leaving. Now do you understand?"

He landed a final, echoing punch against the door. Then silence. Zara lowered herself deeper into the water, her chin dipping below the surface. She curled her arms around her knees, and waited. A minute passed and when no further sound came from beyond the door, she relaxed and stretched out in the luxurious tub. *I guess he took the hint.* Things were taking a lot of weird turns she hadn't expected. Time to get a game plan.

First, Dr. Klein. Then she'd call Pam, ask her advice. Pay another visit to the Flynn office; sign the work order for the contractors; go get the Beamer.

And get the hell out of here.

*

Jorge steered the Mercedes through traffic in downtown Malaga, heading for Ernesto's house on the north side of town where Marlena waited to be picked up. Though an unusual place for her to be, Jorge would never question the decisions or behavior of his employer, cousin or no. Marly had her own life, and entitled to live it how she wanted. The entire Sanchez clan knew that Ernesto held a torch for her, and it seemed right, natural, for them to be drawn together again. They all missed Tristan, but life must go on.

He stopped at a traffic light. As he drummed his fingertips on the wheel to the rhythm of a song on the radio, he scanned the streetscape. Pedestrians crossed the intersection, a mix of people old and young, men and women, dogs on leashes. He looked left, then right, and something caught his eye.

On a concrete bench under the awning of an office tower entrance, sat a woman. She leaned forward with her elbows on her knees and her chin perched atop her clenched fists, looking lost in thought. Her brow wrinkled a little, but in no way detracted from her pretty features. Her long, shapely legs stretched to the ground, terminating in deadly four-inch stilettos.

On impulse, Jorge turned the corner and pulled over. He parked in front of a convenience store that sold cigarettes, candy and sodas. He went to the counter and bought two limonadas, then walked to the front of the tall building. The solemn beauty still rested on the bench, and with two drinks in his hands, he strode up to her.

"Perdoneme, Senorita," he said. "You seem thirsty. Can I offer you something cool to drink?"

At the sound of his voice, she lifted her chin off her hands and swivelled her face toward him, as if being offered drinks from strangers happened every day of her life. She looked him up and down. *"No, gracias,"* she replied, and turned away again.

Jorge edged closer. *"Por favor,* it's quite warm today. I would not want to see you become dehydrated. That would be a shame." He held out the lemonade within arm's reach.

She gave him a second glance. Apparently deciding he looked harmless and genuine enough, she took the proffered bottle. She exhaled and sat back against the bench. *"Gracias,* you are very kind."

"May I?" he asked, indicating the empty spot next to her.

The woman shrugged. *"Por supuesto.* I don't own the bench."

"Life is funny, isn't it?" he said, sitting down, but leaving an appropriate distance between them. "When it gives you lemons, you must make lemonade."

She took a sip of the tart, yet sweet, soda and flashed a grim smile. "How do you know I have lemons?"

"I don't. But I know that I do. And I make the best from what I'm given."

"What's your name?" she asked.

"Jorge Allesandro," he replied with a nod.

She took a second sip as she seemed to size him up then extended her hand. "Ivette Melendez."

"Pleasure to meet you, Senorita Melendez. So what troubles you?"

"My business," she replied after a long pause. "I've made a commitment I won't be able to honor. I could lose everything."

Jorge frowned and nodded. "That's too bad. But you know what I've heard?" He sipped his own drink and looked off in the distance for a moment before continuing. "That you haven't truly lost everything until you lose your sense of humor."

Ivette eyed him curiously then burst out laughing.

"See?" Jorge said. "You haven't lost everything."

When Ivette's laughter calmed down, she took another swallow from her bottle. "And what about you? What lemons do you have?"

Jorge sighed, considering the question. "I have a good life. A comfortable life," he said. "But even comfort can become… boring. You say to yourself, is that all there is? Is there no greater purpose for me?" He shook his head. "Perhaps there isn't."

"Don't say that." Ivette looked at him with a serious countenance. "Perhaps you weren't meant to see it just yet. Perhaps you must make your own purpose."

"Ah." Jorge tipped his lemonade bottle toward her. "Good advice. Perhaps you should take it."

The long-legged lady pursed her glossy lips into an ironic grin. "You are an interesting person, Jorge Allesandro. Have you always been such a *filósofo*… a philosopher?"

"Philosopher?" He chuckled and shook his head. "No. An optimist, *si*. What is stopping you from honoring your business commitment?"

"My partner…disappeared. And so did the money."

Jorge waited for her to continue, but she sat silent for a long minute. "And something else?" he prodded.

"Yes. But I can't talk about it."

"Where is your business?" he asked.

Ivette looked skyward, and thumbed toward the building behind them. "Here. Top floor. Or at least it will be, when I get the money."

"I see. A building like this, rent must be expensive. What kind of business, if I may ask?" When she seemed to hesitate, Jorge added, *"Escucha,* Listen. I know you've never seen me before. You have no reason to tell me anything. But sometimes you just need to say things out loud. And I have no one to tell. So don't be afraid."

She swallowed the last of her lemonade with finality, as though downing a shot to steel herself. She reached into her purse for a business card from her current shop, and handed one to Jorge. "A salon. I quit my old job to open my own salon and spa. I signed the lease, and I owe money. I have to find him."

Jorge took the card and nodded. "Him? Your partner?"

"More than a partner. He—"—she stopped mid-sentence and looked down at her feet—"we were going to be married." She threw her empty soda bottle into the rubbish bin next to the bench. The gesture seemed to illustrate her feelings on the matter. She turned to look squarely at Jorge. "Pathetic, isn't it? I've been dumped. The party's over, and I'm stuck with *la cuenta.*" Ivette stood to leave. "Thank you for the drink. And for listening."

Jorge rose also. "Don't give up on your dreams. Perhaps the party's just starting."

She smiled at him and reached out for a businesslike handshake. "Good advice. Perhaps you should take it."

Chapter Nineteen

Stephane cursed as he shifted the Jag into fourth and accelerated far beyond the speed limit. Zara didn't seem to be working with the plan he'd laid out. She hated him still. The realization made him wince. But while the crowning jewel to the whole affair would be having Zara back as his mate, for lack of a better word, it didn't have to be a deal-breaker. He could still come out on top. He sensed he'd convinced her of his capability to run the Board of Flynn Enterprises, and also that she had no interest, or time, to do so herself. This worked to his advantage.

Perhaps the BMW would be the clincher. Returning it to her, undamaged, might be enough to sway her back on track and seal the deal. The Frenchman better have that car ready, waiting, and in the condition he promised by the time he got there. Or his other five grand wouldn't be forthcoming.

As he turned onto the isolated street in the warehouse district, he saw the tow truck waiting behind the champagne-gold vehicle. *Good*, he thought. At least something appeared to be going right today. He pulled up ahead of both vehicles and parked. He gave the tow truck driver an address and instructed him to hook up. Before leaving, Stephane reached under the front wheel well of the BMW and retrieved the magnetic lock box that held the keys. Wouldn't look right if the thief hadn't had to work hard. He threw the box into his glove compartment and drove away.

*

A sweet, middle-aged man, Dr. Klein wished Zara well and bid goodbye. She thanked him for his kindness and for fitting her appointment into his tight schedule. Many doctors didn't take new patients, especially not on such short notice. She had Pam to thank for that, and after re-dressing in her black leggings, tunic sweater and knee-high boots, she returned to the waiting room where Parminder sat flipping through a magazine. She looked up as Zara approached, and sprang to her feet. Zara smiled, and motioned for them to exit.

They walked side by side to the elevators in silence, and as they descended twelve floors to the lobby, Pam couldn't rein in her curiosity any longer. "Come on Z, I can't stand the suspense. What's the verdict?"

Zara looked at her friend, feeling a strange mix of anxiety and serenity. "It's time to tell you everything. Come on, let's go sit down somewhere."

A coffee shop on the ground floor sufficed and they chose a table by a window that overlooked the bustling downtown.

"Damn straight, it's time," Pam said. "All of it."

Zara told her about El Mirador, about the explosion, about Cruz, and Miguel the rock star. But mostly she talked about Dave. "I met someone wonderful. We have so much in common; he's all I've ever wanted in a guy. He's smart, he's funny…" She held out her cell phone, showing Pam a picture of him taken in Tenerife.

"He's gorgeous," Pam said, finishing Zara's sentence.

Zara nodded. "I wanted to give him all of me, too. Everything. And in a way, I guess I have." She looked at Pam with a sort of Mona Lisa smile.

Knowing intuitively what she meant, the way only a best friend could, Pam's eyes began to fill with tears. "Oh, Z. I'm so thrilled, and scared for you. Where is this guy?"

Zara pocketed her phone. "In Spain. But you know what's funny? He's from here. From Thunder Bay."

"Does he love you? Is he waiting for you?"

Zara looked out the window, as if peering across the Atlantic, asking the same question. "I believe he loves me," she finally said with a certainty that her face didn't quite convey. "But someone else is waiting for him." She shook her head as if trying to jar the little fact loose from her brain and replace it with a new truth. No matter what happened, Zara now knew that she held a tiny piece of Dave inside her, and no auburn-haired Amazon could take that away. Zara explained about the incident in Tenerife and the calls from Stephane.

"Stephane's been helpful, Pam. I thought he'd changed. But he scared the shit out of me this morning. He stayed the night when he promised to keep his distance, and he's trying to win me back for some reason. The sad part is that he's the logical choice of Board President. Would I be crazy to allow it, or crazy not to?"

Pam began to look uncomfortable. "Z, I have something to tell you. I saw your car last night."

Zara blinked. "You mean, where they found it? In some industrial area, I heard."

Pam shook her head, her raven-black hair swinging across her cheeks. "No, I saw someone driving it. He nearly ran me over. About eight o'clock. What time did you hear from the police?"

Zara chewed her lip. "About nine. Or rather, Stephane did."

"You didn't take the call yourself?"

"No."

"You don't think there's something fishy about that?"

The two women stared at each other. "Were the car keys in your condo? Were they missing?" Pam asked.

Zara's brow wrinkled. "I'm not sure. Everything was a mess. Hard to say what was missing besides the obvious stuff."

"Z, think about this. You left everything in good order. Were any other units in your building B & E'd?"

Zara hesitated. "I don't know. Go on," she said.

Pam counted on her fingers. "You get a call from a guy you know to be a conniving, self-serving liar, who has money and connections. Not from the police, or your insurance company, but him."

She tapped a second finger. "Your car is gone, apparently with the keys. And it turns up unharmed? Come on. That never happens."

Third finger. "Now, all of a sudden, the Montreal office is in a shambles, and who's there to save the day? Stephane freaking Vanier." She swallowed hard. "Forgive me if I don't exactly like the man. He hurt you, big time. And he's an opportunist, if he's anything."

Zara fixed her gaze off in the distance. With a determined pull, she drew the straps of her trusty red handbag over her shoulder. Next to Pam, it felt like her closest friend right now. "Pam. I need you to do something. She pushed a ring of keys toward her across the tabletop. "Take the MG. Go to my condo. There's a brown envelope behind the garburetor under the kitchen sink. Bring it to me at the Flynn office. Do you know the way there?"

Pam nodded yes, and closed her hand over the key ring. Zara covered it with her own hand. *"Gracias, amiga."*

*

Bruce Parker left his son with some profound thoughts. *"Parenthood is an experience not to be missed. Look forward to it. Embrace it. Cherish it."*

Dave considered these as he cruised down Rue Sherbrooke, following the GPS readout to the address that Zara's mother had given him. A satellite radio station played a song that seemed to narrate his purpose for being here.

> *All or nothing, love is war;*
> *Take everything, you want some more.*
> *All or nothing, love is war;*
> *Remember who you're fighting for.*

These words resonated within him as he slowed to his destination. He whistled at the attractive exterior of the converted brick building on Avenue Melville. It fit her exactly. Classic and beautiful.

He parked the Mustang and strode up the walkway to the red-doored entrance. Inside the vestibule, he noticed the mail slot with her name on it. He toyed with the idea of leaving her a note, but dismissed it, not knowing when, or if, she would come here. He'd wait awhile then try calling her. He hoped to hell she would answer. His whole body ached. Whether with fatigue, sadness or raw desire, he could not tell. Perhaps all three. It felt like an eternity since he'd held her, made love to her. And he swore it wouldn't be the last. The longer they were apart, the more certain he became that their lives were inextricably bound together. One couldn't survive without the other.

He returned to the car and watched the building for several more minutes. He noted everything he saw, including the movements of anything and anyone along the street. Checking his side mirror, he saw a red sports car pull up several meters behind his Mustang. A brown-skinned girl, maybe five feet tall with long black hair, got out of the car and paced up the walkway to Zara's building.

Dave sat up straight, his fingers on the door handle. When the girl went inside, he leapt from behind the wheel and followed. He bounded up the steps and wrenched open the outer door. At the sudden movement, the girl whirled to face him, the key still in her hand. She stared at him then blinked hard.

"You're Dave," she said, in a voice that expressed both surprise and certainty.

Dave stopped in his tracks. "Yeah. Who are you?"

"I'm Pam, Zara's friend. She showed me your picture."

He exhaled a tense breath. "How is she?" he asked, his fists clenching and unclenching.

Pam's mouth twitched. "You'd better ask her yourself. I'm going to meet her as soon as I'm done here."

Dave gestured to the inner door that Pam hadn't yet unlocked. "I'm coming with you."

"Okay," she said, twisting the key and yanking open the door. "Are you sure you're up to it? You look beat."

Dave grabbed the edge of the door with one hand and held it open. "I'll risk it."

*

Zara arrived at the Montreal office of Flynn Enterprises just after 3:00 p.m. She pondered the idea of coming to work here. Her father had suggested it more than once. It made sense, especially now with the branch in trouble and no one officially at the helm. If not for his sudden death, Zara realized her destiny might well have landed her exactly here.

This time, however, she stood here alone, without Stephane spelling out every step and procedure for her. She felt a fool, placing her trust in the one person who deserved none. Well, all that was about to change. She pushed open the steel and glass door and stepped into the room in confidence.

As she approached his office, Rejean Houle looked up from his desk. "Monsieur Houle?" Zara asked. He nodded. "Je m'appelle Zara Flynn. Pleasure to meet you."

Rejean catapulted from his chair. "Mademoiselle Flynn," he said, a genuine smile illuminating his features. He reached to shake her hand, which Zara accepted heartily. "S'il vous plait, sit down. Likewise, a pleasure to meet you. I'm sorry I missed you on your previous visit."

"Oui, moi aussi." She took off her coat and sat down opposite him. She took a business card from her handbag and placed it on one of the few clear areas of his cluttered desk.

"My condolences about your father. I hadn't met him personally, but I know he was well respected in the industry."

"Merci," Zara replied. "But business, just as life, must go on, oui?" She smiled at the red-haired man, who wore wire-rimmed glasses and seemed to have a challenge keeping the same reddish facial hair in check. Zara couldn't help but like him. He exuded simple honesty and an obvious enthusiasm for his work. It appeared that recent developments had the man swamped, documents and notebooks taking up most of his desktop.

"How are things going?" she asked.

Rejean sighed. "We're managing. The project with PCL is keeping us afloat."

"Yes, I heard. Why has business dropped off? I'd like to hear it from you."

Rejean sank into his chair. "A number of things happened. First, three board members resigned on the same day. Then, we heard that two of our RFPs, Requests For Proposals, were rejected. It came as some surprise, as we fully expected those contracts to move ahead." He shrugged.

Zara nodded, her brain working hard as she assessed the facts. "When did that happen?" she asked.

Rejean scratched his head. "As I recall, it occurred the day after the board fiasco. Everyone here was in shock." He fell silent and folded his hands across his stomach as he leaned back in his chair. "Fortunately, Monsieur Vanier came forward and offered his help."

Zara's ears prickled. "Monsieur Vanier? What kind of help?"

"He offered to serve as interim Board President, and to look into the RFP responses."

"And? What did he find?"

"Nothing yet. But just after that, several employees quit, and we had just enough staff to get by on the remaining contracts."

"And do you know why they quit?"

Rejean nodded. "They all received offers from other companies. Better salaries, benefits."

"What other companies?"

"Strangely enough, not engineering companies, but a law firm. Coté and Associates."

Zara stiffened. "A law firm? Interesting, don't you think?"

"Oui. I thought so."

"Did you realize that Coté & Associates has recently become Coté, Vanier & Associates?"

Houle sat motionless. "Are you sure?"

Zara nodded. The pieces fell into place. The Flynn office had been methodically taken apart. She had no doubt the missing employees and board members would reappear the moment Stephane was in charge.

"Monsieur Houle, I intend to remedy this situation. Now."

As if on cue, the front office doors opened. Stephane walked in, looking around the vacant reception area and continuing on toward Houle's office. He stopped short at the sight of Zara.

"Babe, I'm so glad you're here. I was so worried. I had your car towed to Grant's Auto on Maison Boulevard. Not a scratch on it. But I booked it in for inspection, just in case."

"Thanks," she said, breaking the icy silence that descended over the room. Stephane seemed to sense the cool reception.

"What's wrong?" he asked.

Zara stood. "Nothing more than the last time we visited. Monsieur Houle,"—she gestured to Rejean—"has confirmed everything we heard earlier."

Stephane nodded. "Oui. It's a difficult situation, but not an irreversible one. With the right direction from the board, we can turn this around. In fact, I have several colleagues who are willing to let their names stand for election. We'll need to call an extraordinary meeting, of course. You need to be part of that, Zara. So close to the holidays though, we might have to postpone it until the New Year."

As he flashed his signature, oh-so-charming smile, it became utterly clear to Zara that he'd gotten very, very far in the world on his good looks. He seemed to brighten further as a new thought struck him.

"In that case, we could go up to the cottage for Christmas. It'll be wonderful, just like old times." He sent a deep and meaningful look into Zara's eyes. "We could re-start."

Rejean coughed and rose from his chair. "Excusez-moi, perhaps you should finish this conversation alone," he said as he moved past them toward the door. "Please, use my office." He gave Zara a nod before leaving that signalled he'd be available nearby if she needed him.

"What do you say, sweetheart?" Stephane asked, moving close to her and brushing his hands up and down her arms. "I'm sorry about this morning. I'm moving too fast for you, I see that now. Let's get away for awhile, over the holidays. Just what we need, both of us work too hard."

Zara decided to play along. To catch a thief, you must first become a thief. She placed her hands against his thick chest and pretended to study the lapels of his suit jacket. "I'm the CEO. I have no choice but to work hard." She inhaled the full effect of Hugo Boss, and stroked the fine material beneath her fingertips.

Stephane leaned his head down to rest his chin on her head. His hands left her arms and snaked neatly behind her back. He exhaled with what seemed like relief and Zara sensed the tension leaving him in a peculiar way. *He thinks he's won.*

"All that can be behind you now, babe. I'm here, I'll take care of everything. I'll take care of you."

She winced at his use of Dave's pet name for her. *Babe.* "What if I don't want to be taken care of? I have to work, Stephane. It's my company." She lowered her voice to a teasing tone, hoping to draw him further into his false sense of triumph.

He seemed to rock gently back and forth, holding her in his arms. "Technically, yes. You're the CEO of the European division, but not the North-Am. You'd have to be appointed by the Board. It's a heavy load, babe. You don't need the extra stress. You've enough to carry back in Spain."

Gears shunted and clicked in Zara's head. *He wants to be Board President. The board names the CEO. He could cut me out of the management here with a single vote. How did he think I'd react to that? Smile and play house with him in Collingwood for the rest of my career?* God, she hoped Pam would get here soon.

"Don't call me babe," she said quietly.

Chapter Twenty

"Turn here," Pam said as the Mustang raced along Rue Berri toward Sainte Catherine Street. "You can park underground." She pointed to the underground parking entrance on the south side of the building. Dave cruised down the ramp and pulled into a vacant stall. Deciding to take only one vehicle from Zara's neighborhood, he and Pam hurried to the elevators, their mismatched steps echoing in the cavern of concrete. Dave punched 8 on the panel.

"How'd you know the office was on eight?" Pam asked.

Dave blinked hard "I didn't. Just habit. The Malaga office is on the eighth floor. I pressed it without thinking."

They reached their destination and pushed through the double glass doors in unison. A red-headed man stood in the reception area, startled by their dramatic entrance. "Bonjour, may I help you?" he asked, adjusting his glasses in a way that reminded Dave of Ernesto.

"Dave Parker, from the EU office in Malaga," Dave said, quickly extending a hand to him. "Is Miss Flynn here?"

"Bienvenue, Monsieur Parker. Je suis Rejean Houle, acting Operations Manager." He shook Dave's hand. "I recall your name from the corporate organization charts. Oui, she is in my office with Monsieur Vanier."

Pam made a noise. "Oh, no. What's that rat doing here?"

Dave shot her a look. "Who the fuck is Vanier?"

"Someone you won't like. We'd better get in there."

As they moved toward the closed door, Rejean touched Pam on the arm. "Perhaps you should knock first," he advised.

Pam and Dave exchanged glances. "Like hell," Pam said. "Bust it down."

Dave threw open the door. There, in the greenish glow of fluorescent lighting stood a blond giant of a man with his arms locked around Zara. They both looked toward the door in alarm.

Dave felt blood rising in his neck. *Who the hell is this ape with his arms around my girl?* He focused in on her face, the face that meant everything to him. The one he'd crossed an ocean to find again.

"Dave," she said, her voice sounding faint and far away. She returned his penetrating stare, her green eyes growing wide and dark like those of a trapped animal. He moved without thinking.

"Get your hands off her," he growled, gripping the man's beefy shoulder and shoving him aside.

"Hey," the ape shouted, raising his arm to deflect the blow. "Who do you think you are?"

"You first, asshole." Dave replied.

"Z, are you okay?" Pam's frightened voice cut through the male hostility that permeated the room.

Zara stepped back, unable to take her eyes off Dave. "Never better."

The blond man looked them up and down. "This is a private meeting."

"Answer the question." Dave said. "Who the hell are you?"

The man continued to glare at him, clearly considering himself above such interrogation.

"Pam," Zara interrupted. "Did you bring what I asked?"

"Yup. Right here." She handed Zara an elastic-bound portfolio.

Zara took it and handled its smooth brown surface thoughtfully for a moment. "Some social etiquette is in order," she said. "Stephane Vanier, may I introduce Mr. David Parker and Miss Parminder Singh."

Stephane remained standing near Zara in a protective manner, appearing unimpressed with either of the newcomers. "Friends of yours?" he asked. "Frankly, my dear, I'd have expected better."

Zara's face blushed hot pink as her temper rose. "Is that so?" she retorted. "Well *frankly*, Stephane, I expected nothing better from you, you lying bastard."

Stephane gaped at her. "What are you talking about, babe? I thought we had this all worked out. When have I lied to you? What are these people doing here?"

Dave took a step forward. "I'm warning you, step away from her. And if you value your balls, buddy, don't call her babe." He sized up the man in front of him. Although of similar height, Dave figured the guy had at least fifty pounds on him, and showed no sign of being intimidated.

"Spare me the cowboy antics," Stephane said.

"You lied to me from the beginning," Zara interjected. "My condo wasn't broken into by chance. You arranged it. And you sent my car on a little vacation with a friend of yours. Pam saw him driving it around the night it turned up. How else did you find it so easily and without any damage? A smokescreen, all of it, to lure me back here and trick me into naming you to the Board of Directors."

"The company's in trouble, Zara. I'm offering it a way out. I have no other motive than that."

"Sounds like bullshit to me," Dave said, his eyes narrowing.

Stephane relaxed his stance, and moved back a pace. He raised both hands in a halting gesture. "This is ridiculous. You can't come in here, uttering threats. You'd better leave, or I'll have security remove you both."

"There's only one person leaving, Stephane. And that's you," Zara said. She opened the portfolio and withdrew a sheaf of papers. "You say I'm not the CEO of this division, but this document clearly says otherwise. My father's will. You don't seem to have read it thoroughly."

"I've read it," Stephane said darkly. "And it makes you subject to the Board's decisions like any other CEO."

"True. But the terms of succession give me the ability, in extenuating circumstances, to supercede any Board decision, worldwide. Even as President, I could quash any motion you present. In short, you have no power without me. Now get out."

Stephane bristled, anger settling over his countenance like a shroud. He fixed them all with a haughty stare, and tilted his chin toward Dave. "You think I don't know who you are? I've made it my business to know all of the company personnel. You're an over-achieving science major from Buttfuck, Ontario who lucked out getting a job with an international construction giant. Ambitious. Looking to move up in the company." His face twisted into an evil grin. "What better way to climb the corporate ladder than to screw the heiress after its CEO drops dead?" He swung his glance to Zara. "You didn't see it coming, did you, sweetheart? At least I'm trying to pilot the company with my brains and not my dick."

Zara paled at Stephane's crude words. A curtain of red passed over Dave's eyes. He'd only met the man a few minutes ago, yet already hated him with every fibre of his soul. He wanted nothing more at this moment than to get his hands around Stephane's throat. His fingers twitched at the prospect.

"I said get out," Zara repeated, her voice betraying the tears filling her eyes.

"You can't tell me what to do. I'm already serving on the board," Stephane said.

"You'll never be sworn on as President," Zara said coldly. Her hands shook as she tried to shove the papers back into the portfolio.

Stephane cocked his head to one side. "And who is going to stop me? The Lone Ranger here?" he pointed at Dave. "And Tonto?" His gaze slipped over Pam.

That's it. This ape is going down. Stephane stood about a foot away from the wall, his attention directed toward Pam. Perfect. Dave lined him up in his sights, imagining the wall behind Stephane as a rinkboard. With a lunging stride, he nailed him in a crushing bodycheck.

Stephane's head whipped back and banged into the wall with a sickening crack. Pam let out a shriek. Dave saw Stephane's eyes roll back as his heavy frame slid downward. He gave him an extra shove to land him in a heap at the baseboards.

"Not the Lone Ranger." Dave said. "More like a New York Ranger."

Pam screamed again. She rushed forward and crouched down next to Zara, who lay on the floor, unconscious. Dave stepped over Stephane's motionless form to join them.

"She fainted," Pam said, placing her fingers to Zara's throat in search of her pulse. "She's not well. We have to get her out of here."

Dave needed no further urging. In a heartbeat, he scooped Zara's body from the carpet. He murmured the same words she'd said to him on the darkened shores of the Mediterranean what felt like aeons ago. "Okay, Lightning Girl, snap out of it, need your help here."

Pam opened the door to see Rejean rushing toward his office at the sound of the commotion within. He stood aside as Dave carried Zara into the hallway and laid her on a couch in the reception area. "Get some water."

"I'm on it," Pam said, sprinting to the water cooler at the far end of the room.

"C'mon, babe. Wake up," Dave whispered, brushing her hair from her forehead.

Pam returned with a paper cup and held it to Zara's lips. "Z, drink this," she urged. Zara's head began to move and she opened her mouth to accept the water. She managed a small sip before it ran down the sides of her jaw. Her eyes opened partway and focused on Dave's face hovering over her. The tip of her tongue slipped out to lick the beads of moisture from her white-rimmed lips.

"Thunder Boy," she said weakly. "Are you really here?"

Dave exhaled in relief, an anxious smile quirking one side of his mouth. "Afraid so, mademoiselle. And I'm not leaving."

Zara closed her eyes again. "Good."

"Here's her coat and bag," Pam said, placing the shiny red tote on the floor next to the couch. "I'll hang on to the documents, for safekeeping. Take her home now, she needs rest. Tell her I'll call her later." She stood to leave. "Nice hit, by the way. Defenceman, huh?"

Dave regarded her curiously. "Once upon a time. Where are you going? Aren't you coming with us?"

Pam shook her head, and tossed him the keys Zara had given her. "Nuh-uh. You two have a lot of talking to do. And I don't wanna be here when Shit-head wakes up." She thumbed toward the hallway leading to Houle's office. "I suggest you do the same." She turned on her heel and left, her raven hair swishing behind her.

Dave stared after her for a second, until Zara began to stir. "It's not true, is it?" she said, her voice barely above a whisper. "Screwing your way to the top?" Her eyes looked glazed.

"You know it's not," he scolded her. "Hang on to me." He'd have to let Houle deal with Shit-head. Dave lifted her from the couch and curled her body tight against his chest. She felt so light, weighing almost nothing in his arms. He wondered what Pam meant by "she's not well." He cursed himself for not getting here sooner. He moved her carefully out of the office, into the elevator and down to the parking level, setting her on her feet as they reached the Mustang.

"Nice wheels, Thunder Boy." She spoke as if in a dream state, and it worried him.

"Glad you like it. Let's get you inside." He opened the passenger door and folded her delicate frame into the front seat. The air temperature in the parking garage seemed even colder than the outdoors. Dave draped her coat over her before climbing into the drivers' side.

"Mmm, comfy," she murmured. She looked on the verge of sleep. Something told him this wasn't a good sign, and decided he should keep her talking.

He leaned over and tucked the coat close around her. Damn, she looked beautiful. Every inch of his body ached with wanting to hold her. Hell, he wanted much more than that. "Are you okay?" were all the words he could muster.

Zara opened her eyes fully and looked at him as if seeing him for the first time. A pale hand reached out from under the coat and grabbed his shirt, pulling him closer. "Okay? Okay?" Her hand moved to slip behind his neck. "If that's all you've got, Mr. Smart-Ass, shut up and kiss me."

She pulled his head forward until their lips met in a kiss so hungry it caught him off-guard. Emotions he'd been holding back for so many days surfaced in a sizzling rush. His every limb felt made of molten lava as he enveloped her in a fiery embrace. She seemed to mold herself to his body as he did so, her kisses more and more urgent. He felt his erection pressing painfully against his jean zipper, and knew he wouldn't be able to contain himself for very long. Her reaction to him didn't help. She hoisted herself higher on the seat, climbing over the console between them and wedging herself in his lap.

The cabin of the Mustang didn't offer much room, but it mattered not. Their surroundings seemed to fall away, leaving nothing but their desire for one another to fill the space. He hadn't pictured their reunion in quite this way.

"Zara," he started, in between her fervent kisses. "Babe." Another kiss. He chuckled in delight at her attentions. "This isn't exactly a good place—"

She smothered his words with another kiss. "I said, shut up. It's perfect. We're alone where no one will find us. Like a lunar capsule in space." She undid the buttons on his shirt and roved her hands over the taut skin of his chest.

God. His dick grew harder as she continued to kiss him. Her body rubbed against the bulge in his jeans making it worse. "Hello to you, too," he said, when she finally drew back for breath.

"Hello," she whispered. Her eyes glistened with tears that threatened to spill down her cheeks. "I'm so sorry. About everything. I had no right to judge you, and I don't care about your past. I love you. And you came for me, so you must love me, too. I need to hear you say it."

She was right. He'd never openly spoken those words to her. The closest he came was in a text message, and once in the blinding moments of fucking the daylights out of her. How incredibly lame. She deserved so much better. He brought his hands to either side of her face and held her head steady so that she had no choice but to look into his eyes when he said it this time. "Zara Flynn, listen carefully. *I...love...you*, do you hear? I love you. And I'm never going to let you go."

He barely got the sentence out before she was kissing him again, her tongue seeking his, as if to suck the words from his mouth and swallow them, to keep them inside her forever. He reached down to ease the seat back and provide more room. The windows had already begun to fog up. A parking lot fuck? What the hell, he felt crazy as a teenager right now, his loins on fire. Her fingers were undoing his jeans and pulling on the zipper.

"Babe, are you sure you want to do this? Pam said you weren't well. I said I wouldn't ever hurt you, and..."—he swallowed hard—"I don't have any protection with me."

She smiled, and pushed his jeans down lower, releasing his throbbing cock. "It doesn't matter." She took hold of his shaft, stroking it. His pre-cum oozed down over her fingers. "I want you to hurt me," she said, her voice taking on a surreal, purring tone. "Hurt me good."

Rational thought left Dave's mind completely. He slipped his fingers under the waistband of her leggings and pushed the form-fitting material down over her hips, his palms gliding over her round buttocks. She flexed like a cat to slide her tall boots off, allowing him to push her bottoms past her knees and onto the floor. He felt dizzy as her earthy scent filled his nostrils. Jesus, he had to get inside her or he'd lose his mind.

Her breasts pressed against him as she raised up on her knees, straddling him. He slipped his hands around the back of her thighs and stroked the soft skin, feeling it prickle into goosebumps. His touch slid upward to her crotch, dipping his fingers into the soft lips of flesh around her entrance that were wet and hot for him. The sensation drove his arousal even higher.

Zara moaned and shuddered as his fingertips touched her clit, sliding forward and back again, pressing, squeezing and tapping in succession. The slippery tissue seemed to swell and writhe between his fingers and, by her rapid little cries, knew he'd found her magic spot. He rubbed the head of his dick back and forth against her well-primed slit a few times before pushing in. Her cries descended into a low groan as she let herself down upon him, matching his upward thrusts.

He lost himself inside her, his hands gripping her buttocks as they bounced up and down, smacking the tops of his thighs with each stroke. The scents of patchouli and sex swirled in his consciousness until oblivion beckoned, and he surged into climax with her body pounding against his. He let everything go.

"Give it to me, Thunder Boy…hurt me, fuck me raw. You belong to me."

The sound of his own heaving breath clouded his hearing. Did she speak those words or did he just imagine it? He liked the sound of them either way. Several moments passed as their bodies stilled, and heartbeats decelerated. Condensation ran in miniature rivers down the inside of the window glass.

"We can't stay here much longer." Dave said. "Let me take you somewhere. Anywhere."

Zara clung to him with her arms around his neck and her chin resting on top of his tousled head. "I'd like that. Take me home."

Chapter Twenty-One

Stephane eased himself out of his Jag, his knees stiff and his right shoulder bruised and throbbing. He dared not move his head left or right, the pain in his neck so intense. He pressed a button on his key fob and heard the familiar double chime of the alarm system activating. In the gathering dusk, he moved stiffly toward the back entrance of his office building. The fair-sized goose egg on his head pulsed miserably with each step, reminding him what a total fuck-up his day had turned out to be.

Options. He needed options now that Zara's personal cavalry had arrived. He still held the cards as far as staffing and project contracts went. Even if he wasn't elected to the Board, the fact remained that, thanks to him, Flynn Enterprises North America had no upcoming work, and no staff to execute it if there were. And it would remain that way until he got what he wanted: control of the company. One way or another.

His head hurt like hell, thanks to the punk-ass engineer. He wondered what sort of charm he could possibly have cast over Zara that would make a girl like her look at him twice. Stephane punched the security code on the keypad and entered the building. He'd have preferred to sleep in his own house, but for the moment, the executive suite attached to his office would have to suffice. He ignored the service lift in favour of the secure elevator to which he had the only key. The doors opened on command and he stepped in. The lift went straight to the top floor, and he limped painfully to the suite's entrance.

A few hours sleep, and he'd be able to think this thing out, like he always did. He entered a second key code and the light turned green. He twisted the lever and pushed the heavy door open, his shoulder protesting in pain. He lurched across the threshold and, balancing most of his weight on one foot, let it fall shut behind him.

He sniffed the air inside the dark room. It smelled funny. Like someone had smoked a cigar recently. He'd just been in here two days ago, what the fuck? Before his instincts could kick in, he felt a heavy blow to his shins that dropped him to his knees. Then another against his back, sending him face down on the carpet. He vaguely heard footsteps shuffling near him and a few words of muttered French, before he blacked out.

*

"Now what do we do with him?" Carlos asked, the wooden lamp base he'd struck the intruder with, still in his hand. He and Alain stood over Stephane's crumpled bulk in the darkened room.

"*Stupide!* Finish him off or run like hell. Either way you're in shit, ami. No place for you to go, now."

"There has to be someplace. You must know every dive in this frozen town."

"Merde!" Alain cursed. "I not your babysitter. We just robbed his office, can't hang around for your sake. Hit him again. *Vamos.*"

Carlos bit his lip, and shifted the lamp from his right hand to his left. "I've never killed anyone before."

Alain snorted in disgust. "You mean, not by your own hand. The stuff you peddle kills plenty, Monsieur Bigshot. Do it, and I get you out of here." He moved toward the door as if to leave Carlos behind.

Carlos tightened both hands on the lamp, braced his footing, and swung. The wood splintered as it connected with Stephane's head. Carlos let the pieces fall to the floor then rushed out the door after Alain.

The two men took the stairs, bolting down flight after flight until they reached the ground floor and the exit. Darkness shielded them as they stepped outside.

"Where to now?" Carlos asked.

"Not together. You go first, cross that alley, turn right, onto the next street. I be right behind you." As Carlos hurried toward the alley, Alain slipped his cell phone from his pocket and took a photo of Carlos' retreating backside. Alain followed a few moments later, meeting up with him behind a city bus shelter on the next block. Dim light filtered through the shelter's grimy plexiglass panels. Any emotion Carlos felt remained hidden behind the man's olive complexion and Van-Dyke style beard.

"I give you an address," Alain said. "Don't go there until I tell you." Again he used his cell phone, and thumbed the keypad as though searching though his contacts. "Go to Café Paris, on Sainte-Catherine and Crescent. Wait there."

"How long will you be?"

"I have to arrange things with a friend first. Could be an hour, could be five minutes. Have an espresso. You need it. Go that way,"—Alain pointed—"turn left and take Sainte-Catherine to Crescent. On the corner, can't miss it."

Carlos nodded and turned to follow his instructions. Alain pressed the capture button once more then walked in the opposite direction. The image looked a bit motion-blurred, but recognizable as a man on the run. He grunted in satisfaction and put the phone away.

*

A single candle lit the bay window facing Avenue Melville. The table next to the window had been set with what unbroken dishes Zara could find, mismatched silverware, and brandy snifters that would have to double as wine glasses for the evening. The original wood-burning fireplace, retrofitted for natural gas, supplied a romantic, flickering glow at the flip of a switch.

"Are you sure you want to stay here tonight?" Dave asked. "We could get a hotel, you know. Get a massage, have a bubble bath, order room service? Pam said you needed rest."

Zara filled a saucepan of water from her kitchen sink, surrounded by the mess left behind by the break-in. "No way," she answered. "I owe you a dinner. You're not the only one who can cook." She turned to face him as he wrapped his arms around her.

"I'd hardly call spaghetti and meat sauce 'cooking'," he said. "But after a day like today, even peanut butter and jam would sound like a gourmet meal."

"Good. Because it might be all that's left in the cupboard after the spaghetti's gone."

"Seriously, babe." He lifted her to sit on the counter, and pressed her thighs open with his hips. The rough denim brushed against her skin. "Are you sick? Tell me what the hell's been going on."

Zara looked into those cobalt-blue eyes she adored, wishing she could drown in them. She ran her fingers through his wavy hair, grown longer than she'd ever seen it. He'd obviously had other things on his mind lately than visiting his hairstylist. As thrilled as she was that he'd come after her, burning questions filled her mind.

"You heard most of it already. Stephane Vanier is a self-centered, manipulative bastard. You could be in trouble. He's a lawyer and could have you up on assault charges after today. He's the one who contacted me when we were in Tenerife. I didn't know that it was all a set-up, to get me back here and trick me into giving him control of the Montreal office."

"Why would you listen to him? Why did you let him… touch you that way." His lips tightened and the blue eyes closed as if trying to block out the memory of the scene he'd stumbled upon in the Flynn office.

Zara put her arms around his neck and held him close. "Please. It wasn't what it looked like, you have to believe me. I hate him. I was trying to trap him, catch him in his lies."

"By seducing him? That's a pretty old trick." Dave's voice hardened. "I wouldn't have expected that from you."

Zara winced. *He doesn't believe me.* Her heart constricted at the thought she might lose him over all this, at a time when she'd realized beyond all doubt how she felt about him. She took a deep breath in.

"You said it yourself. Everyone has a past. Unfortunately, Stephane was part of mine. You were right, we can't punish each other for the past. We can only change the future." She rested her forehead against his. "So I need to know. Is…that woman…in your future?" Her throat went dry as she chose her next words. Her voice cracked, and tears stung her eyes as she spoke them. "Are you the father of her child?"

There. She'd let the words out, where they floated in the air like weighted balloons. She felt his body quiver in her embrace.

"Oh, Zara," he said, his voice almost a sob. He breathed in and out a few times, to regain his composure. "I can tell you that I believe, with all my heart and soul, that I am not. And that I will take any measures to prove it. And that it will not change my feelings, or my intentions, toward you. You are with me, in my heart, in my mind, in my soul. As I hope I am in yours."

His words ripped through her like a hot knife. There could be no mistake now, they were bonded to each other in every way that mattered. Zara felt something release within her, and tears streamed down her face. Her insides seemed to twist and buck in a mixture of joy and fear. "You are in me, my love," she said. "More than you know."

Water spilled over from the pot she'd set to boil for the pasta. The hissing noise startled them both, and they jerked away from each other. Zara reached for the controls and switched the burner off. "Are you still hungry?" she asked.

Dave appeared shaken as he stood back from her and the stove. The steam rose in a cloud between them, as he looked at her with an almost frightening intensity. "Yeah. But not for spaghetti."

"It can wait," Zara said. She sat on the counter top, her bare feet dangling like a lost girl in a playground. His arms went around her again, and lifted her off the granite surface. Her legs wrapped around his back as he carried her to the adjoining room. They tumbled onto the floor in front of the fireplace, atop scattered magazines, books and cushions.

The warmth of the flames caressed their already heated bodies. "We're going to starve to death, aren't we?" he said. "In a city full of great restaurants."

"But what a way to go," she answered, and they both began to laugh. As they lay together in the flickering light of the fire, he stroked her hair and gazed into her face, seeming to struggle for any further words. Zara spoke first. "I'm done here. I miss the sun, and the sea. Let's go home tomorrow."

Dave's hands stopped moving. "I thought this was your home. You said so when you left me at the airport."

Her lips retracted into a thin line, then relaxed again. "I was wrong. The longer I stay here, the more I realize what I really came here to do. Close a door. This place represents…a life I no longer live."

They fell silent for several moments, the meaning of her words sinking in. "So what happens to this apartment?" he asked.

"I'll sell it. My car, too. Montreal means nothing to me, anymore."

"What about the Flynn operations here?"

Zara shook her head. "I'm not sure. But I'll figure it out, somehow."

Dave smiled, and placed his hand behind her head, pulling her into his chest. "That's the Lightning Girl I know. Invincible." She clung to him, willing her body to meld with his, become one. "I have a surprise for you," he whispered. "When we get back."

Zara squeezed him tighter, alerting her senses to his every muscle and curve. A rush of heat swept through her, settling between her legs. "I have a surprise for you, too. And I don't think it can wait until we get back."

He pulled his head back, enough to look into her eyes. "What?"

It was all or nothing, now. She inhaled a steady breath.

"I'm pregnant."

Chapter Twenty-Two

Alain counted the cash from the envelope Vanier had given him the week before. Five thousand, in older bills. Better than nothing, but only half of what Vanier promised. *Poor dumb shit.* Would have been better if he'd died. However, dead or alive, the situation had two redeeming factors. He came away with a very nice cache of stolen goods, and he could still sink Sabados. He headed for the public library. The computers there wouldn't leave a trail, and he could upload his photos and forward his anonymous news tip from there. He thought about the Spaniard waiting for his call, and couldn't decide who was dumber, the Spaniard or the Lawyer.

*

It bit him. The dolphin's pointed jaws closed around his hand in a swift lunging attack, then released it and swam off, giving an insolent flip of its tail. He expected his hand to bleed and sting, yet it remained whole and unmarked. The dolphin's body disappeared into the dark depths below, leaving a sinuous trail of bubbles. Dave swam upward, toward the light; the nearer he got, the more difficult it seemed to break the surface. Something held him back. He clawed at the circle of bright water, unable to send even a fingertip into the air above. He panicked. He felt something slick swipe across his foot, and looking down, saw the dolphin gliding below him, circling and brushing up against him. Its black eyes glinted in the murky abyss. He tried for the water's surface again, when he suddenly felt lifted from below. The damn thing had swum underneath him, forcing him to ride its back like an aquarium trainer.

It rose higher, bringing him closer to the precious circle of light that meant salvation. They surfaced, and sped toward the shore in a spray of water and waves. He pitched forward, landing face-first while the dolphin slipped away with the receding surf. He lay prone on the hard, wet beach, struggling for air as he spat out seawater and grains of sand that filled his mouth.

He coughed, and opened his eyes to reality. Alone in a bed, in a room he didn't recognize. Blood thundered in his ears like remnants of the ocean from his dream. He growled in anger, wondering when in holy hell the vile creature would leave his dreams in peace. As his breathing slowed, his surroundings became clear—Zara's condo on Avenue Melville. But he lay there alone.

He righted himself off the mattress, his eyes searching the room for her. Her words echoed in his brain. *I'm pregnant.* A thousand emotions ran through him; happiness, fear, anticipation, awe. He wanted this with her, yet somehow felt he'd cheated, robbed her of the joy of her announcement. Where had she gone? He heard water running, and his panic eased. Rubbing the sleep from his eyes, he rose and crept to the bathroom.

*

Bubble-clouds danced on the surface of the bath water as Zara stretched out in the tub. She closed her eyes and inhaled the delicious fragrances of melon and coconut that rose from them. She heard footsteps approaching, and the familiar creak of her wooden bathroom door. She opened her eyes to see Dave standing there in the nude, all tanned skin and sculpted muscle on display. No tattoos marred his arms or shoulders. Nothing to obscure the view of his youthful, athletic body, from the muscled calves to the tight cords of his neck. And in between, his smooth chest, well-defined abs, and unreasonably cute belly button called out for attention. Her eyes followed the feathery field of hair that began just below his navel and thickened into a soft forest surrounding his impressive cock. Although not a new sight, it still made her insides go hot just looking at him.

"Hi," he said. "Everything okay?"

Zara doused the lusty thoughts forming in her brain. She nodded, the sound of his voice making her smile. "Oui, Monsieur. Care to join me?"

His slow advance toward her, stark naked and in full daylight, was possibly the sexiest thing she'd ever seen. She raised her eyes to his face, and he tilted his head as if questioning her stare. A swath of hair fell across his forehead and over one eye as he did so, making him seem charmingly boyish. The slow-burning smile that she'd come to know so well began its progress across his lips, his adorable dimples forming along with it. They creased his angular jaw, accentuating the day's worth of beard that covered it in just the right places. God, she could eat him up.

Zara leaned forward and wrapped her arms around her knees, making room for him to step into the bath behind her. The water level rose as he slipped down into the water, leaning his chest in tight against her back, and drawing his knees around either side of her. The sloshing water licked at them, leaving daubs of bubbles sticking to their skin. He pulled her wet hair aside and kissed the nape of her neck. His cock pressed against her bottom. She shivered.

He said nothing, but reached for the shower puff and tube of gel on the tub ledge. Squeezing a few drops onto the puff, he stroked it across the wet skin of her back. Down, then up, across and down, up in a circle around her shoulder blades, over the little bump on the back of her neck. She reveled in his touch, and the fact that even this simple motion could get her aroused as hell. No matter that they'd been making love all night, she felt ready for him all over again. She hoped that wouldn't stop in the months to come.

"Will you still rub my back like this when I'm big and fat?" she asked.

He kept scrubbing in the same steady motion. "Nope. I'll do it even better."

Zara giggled. "I'll hold you to that." She concentrated on the gentle passes of the shower puff, enjoying every second of it. Dave hadn't seemed shocked when she broke the news to him. Quite the opposite. The look of pure joy and unabashed tears in his luscious blue eyes when she told him made her breathe a silent prayer of thanks. But, at the moment, this uncharacteristic absence of words disturbed her.

The puff plopped down in front of her. He began smoothing handfuls of bath water over her to rinse off the suds. Even this innocent contact sent bolts of desire through her, and her breathing elevated. When he touched the back of her neck, his motion stopped.

"Where's your necklace?" he asked.

Zara thought for a second. "The coral one?"

"No, the silver one."

She recalled the morning at Stephane's house. "The chain broke. I lost it." *Why did he want to know?*

At his continued silence, the bath water began to feel chill, quelling her body's rising need for him. "We have a big day, we should get going."

He cupped her breasts. "Not yet. Breakfast first."

"We'll have to get out of the tub for that."

"Not for this kind of breakfast." He rolled her nipples between his thumb and forefingers.

She tilted her head back, trying to ignore the urgent tingling in her breasts. No good. They hardened into little pebbles and she sighed in surrender. "Don't forget, I'm eating for two, then."

His hands slid down around her thighs and in between her legs, nudging them apart. "I like the sound of that," he said, fingertips sliding toward her center beneath the sweet-smelling bubbles.

The red handbag lay on the floor in the empty bedroom, and the repeated buzzing of Zara's phone inside it went unheeded.

*

Zara prepared to say goodbye to the apartment on Avenue Melville as she packed a few last belongings. She felt no regret at leaving now, convinced that her true future lay elsewhere. Montreal had never been kind to her. The more she considered this, the faster she seemed to move. Suddenly nothing seemed as important as getting away from this place.

She went for her phone to see what flights they could book. Between them, she and Dave had decided to return to Tenerife and pick up their interrupted vacation where they left off. She plucked the phone from her bag, and swore aloud. "Shit. I forgot to charge this. Dead as nails." She dug for her charger in another bag, and plugged in.

Dave joined her in the living room with his knapsack slung over one shoulder. *"Que pasa?"* he asked as she scrolled through the list of calls.

"The Flynn office," she said, casting him an ominous glance. She punched the reply, and got Houle on the line.

"Mademoiselle Flynn, are you all right? I've been trying to reach you."

"Tres bien, thank you for your concern. Please let me apologize for causing such an unpleasant incident yesterday. I do plan to resolve the situation."

"I'm sure you will, Miss." Houle paused. "But I'm afraid I have some bad news." He cleared his throat before continuing. "Monsieur Vanier's office called. There's been a robbery, and he didn't show up for his appointments this morning. They found him in the executive suites, unconscious. He's been attacked, and they've taken him to the hospital."

Zara felt the room start to shrink around her. "Oh, my God." Her throat tightened, unable to respond further. Dave looked over in concern.

"The last they heard from him, he was on his way to our office yesterday. That's why they called. I told them he left here around four o'clock, but didn't go into detail. I'm afraid the situation won't look good for Mr. Parker if the police start to investigate. I don't mean to suggest anything, but can you tell me where you and Mr. Parker went last night after you left?"

Zara swallowed, summoning enough moisture in her mouth to speak. "We went to my apartment. On Avenue Melville. We're still here, in fact." She ran her tongue over her dry lips. *I need to know.* "What is his...Mr. Vanier's, condition? Is he all right?" Dave shot her a 'what the hell?' look.

Rejean took a breath. "Critical, I'm afraid. Trauma to the head, I'm told. But, I assure you, he left here under his own power. A little bruised, perhaps. Mostly his ego, I think. What happened in there? I'd like to...as you said...hear it from you."

"I have reason to believe Mr. Vanier is seeking control of the Board for his own gain. He also made some disparaging remarks, racial slurs toward my friend. Mr. Parker took offense to these actions and…became physical. He defended us." She paused, thinking about the situation she'd left Houle in. "If the police do question you, Rejean, please be truthful. We have nothing to hide. I'll keep in touch." She disconnected and set the phone down to continue charging. "Stephane's in hospital."

Dave lifted one eyebrow. "He deserves it."

Zara shook her head. "No, not like that. Someone attacked him in his office last night, during a robbery. He's in critical condition."

Chapter Twenty-Three

Zara and Dave stopped at Grant's Auto and paid for the inspection of the BMW before heading to the airport. Dave insisted that Zara eat, so they met Pam for brunch, where Zara handed her a key and a folded pink paper.

"What's this?" Pam asked, her eyes widening in query.

"Got a loonie on you?" Zara asked.

"A loonie? Why?"

"Because I've signed the registration as sold to you for a dollar. The Beamer's yours. You can keep it, or sell it. Consider it your commission for listing my condo."

Pam looked at her silently. "Z, that's too much. I can't take your Beamer."

Zara closed her hands around Pam's as she clutched the keychain. "You can, and you will. I insist."

Pam's lips formed a stubborn pout. "I'll do it only because you've asked me to. But it feels so final. Am I ever going to see you again?"

Zara smiled at her friend. "Of course you will. In fact, why don't' you come and see me, next time? In Spain. I'll book your ticket whenever you say."

"How about when baby is born?" Pam winked at both of them.

Dave rubbed Zara's back at these words. "Consider it done," he answered for her.

"I'm on shift at the hospital tonight," Pam said. "I can check on, you know who. I feel terrible calling him Shit-head now. Sounds like he's hurt bad."

"They might question you about yesterday afternoon. You're an eyewitness."

Pam nodded solemnly. "Well, I can only tell them what I saw."

*

Just after five p.m., Ivette folded towels and stacked them at all the wash stations on her last day at the Bella Spa. She refilled all the product bottles in the back, and stocked all the retail shelves in the front. She'd volunteered to close up the shop for the day, so she wouldn't have to face everyone's long good-byes.

The other stylists congratulated her on her new business, asked her keep in touch. She couldn't tell any of them that her plans had changed, or indeed, may never even happen. She'd kept a straight face, too self-centered to admit defeat in public, but her determination and optimism of a few weeks ago had weakened, along with her resolve to book her medical visit to Amsterdam. Her pocketbook just wasn't looking that good.

She turned on the wall-mounted TV in the customer lounge for some background noise. At this hour, the international news channel sprang to life, but having no intention of watching, she began to turn away when a familiar face flashed on the screen. Ivette froze. She focused on the Spanish captioning that translated the English voiceover.

"...identified as Juan Carlos Sabados, wanted for trafficking crimes in Europe. Apprehended at a Montreal coffee house, an anonymous tip placed Sabados at the scene of the robbery, and is also a suspect in the assault on prominent local lawyer, Stephane Vanier, found critically injured in the adjoining executive suite. After the hearing, Sabados is expected to be extradited to his home country within a few days to face charges..."

Carlos would be coming home...alive. Headed straight for jail, most likely, but alive. Ivette exhaled a breath she didn't realize she was holding. Her heart seemed divided into two halves, one horrified at the bad news, and the other rising in crazy hope that she'd be with him again soon. That he'd return to witness the birth of his child.

Ivette straightened. That this thought had entered her mind took her aback. She hadn't planned to give birth at all, let alone assume she and Carlos might continue life together as a family. She looked around the empty salon, her senses racing. Her life would feel just as empty if she didn't try to make a success of herself, with or without Carlos. And even emptier if she ignored this chance to have a child. Perhaps she'd never be able to have another.

If she could just get the money, she could still open her new business, pregnant or not. Lots of women did. Just then it struck her as a challenge, to run a successful business and raise a child at the same time. Ivette never backed away from a challenge. Now, her course seemed clear. She would get the money somehow.

The door chime sounded. With a sigh of frustration, Ivette realized she hadn't yet locked the entrance. She turned away from the TV, about to shout *"estamos cerrados,"* when her mouth froze open.

The last person she ever expected to see again stood there in the doorway. She blinked in surprise, and felt a smile spread over her face. "Well, if it isn't *El Filósofo,*" she said. "What a surprise."

Jorge grinned, looking quite uncomfortable. Ivette thought it amusing. She hadn't met anyone so utterly unaware of his own charm. She tilted her head questioningly. "What are you doing here?"

Jorge cleared his throat. "I decided I needed a haircut. You do that here, *si?*"

Ivette nodded. "And you just happened to come across this shop?"

He stood with his grin stuck in place for a few awkward seconds. "You gave me your card, remember?"

Ivette raised her eyebrows. "That's right, I did." She stepped toward one of the stylists chairs and patted the headrest, indicating for him to sit.

Jorge cleared his throat. "I was thinking about you a lot, your *situación,* I mean. I thought, I might be of some help, so I…"

As his voice faded off, she patted the chair again, and he obediently sat down. She pivoted the chair toward the mirror, both their faces reflected in it as she stood behind him. The more she looked, the more she found attractive about him. He had a well-shaped face, symmetrical. Squarish chin, not too wide nor pointed. An aquiline, almost regal, sort of nose. His ginger-brown eyes held a brightness that said he had seen much in his lifetime. How old…35, 45? She couldn't guess.

She reached for a comb and set to work on his hair. Thick and curly, there were no signs of gray in it. "You hardly know me. Why should you help me? And anyway, you already know I need a lot of money."

Facing the mirror seemed to lessen Jorge's nervousness. He had no difficulty maintaining eye contact this way, and Ivette found his gaze remarkably intense.

"Lo se. How much do you need?" he asked without blinking.

*

The big jet touched down at Los Rodeos airport on Tenerife's north coast. The jolting rumble of the flaps meeting the runway lifted Zara's head off Dave's shoulder. For the first time, she'd slept almost an entire flight, and smiled at awakening not only to sunny skies, but the comforting scents of leather, denim and Lacoste cologne that he wore.

As the aircraft came to a stop, Zara switched on her phone. A number of calls began to download on the screen, mostly from Marlena. She hit the reply button and waited for her mother to answer.

After three rings, Marlena picked up. Longer than usual.

"Hola?" came the response, in a somewhat sleepy tone.

"Mom?" Zara asked, puzzled.

"Oh, Zara darling. Where are you?"

"I've just landed in Tenerife. We're going to finish our vacation. What are you up to? Did I wake you?"

"No, *querida."* Marlena's voice vibrated in a tender chuckle. "I'm quite all right. I take it David is with you?"

"Yes. Everything's fine. We'll be home at the end of the week. We...need some time alone." She grabbed Dave's hand as they walked through the pedway into the arrivals area. "How are you doing? I've been thinking, we can't stay at the Club forever. We need to find a more permanent home. And Jorge, too."

Marlena laughed aloud. *"Si,* I agree. Why don't you build one?"

"My thoughts exactly." Zara smiled, grateful for the intuitiveness she and her mother shared. "There's room enough to build two villas. So, tell Ernesto to hurry up with prepping the El Mirador site. When you see him next."

"*Si.* I'll do that. Call me with your flight details, so I can send Jorge to get you."

The phone signaled another call waiting. "Thanks, Mom. Adios." They'd reached the baggage carousel, and Zara threw Dave an exasperated look as she pressed the call answer.

"*Hola,* Senorita Flynn? This is Roberta Diaz, the estate agent in Puerto de la Cruz. We spoke last week?"

"Si, I remember you, Senora Diaz." How could she forget the obstinate woman who had no answers to her questions about the old restaurant building? "What can I do for you?"

"Well, if you are still interested, there may be something I can do for you."

"Oh? What's that?"

"The port authority has changed the inspection clause on the property you inquired about. I've been trying to reach you. They are willing to waive the inspection if you can make an offer in the next 48 hours. Unfortunately that was yesterday and you're down to 12 hours now."

Zara's heart leapt. An omen, that she'd made the right decision in returning to Spain. Everything seemed to be falling in place. "I'm interested. But I'll want to see the place, close-up. We weren't able to go inside before. Can someone meet us there, and take us to your office to close the deal if all goes well?"

"I'll make some calls. We close at eight, but I can make some after-hours arrangements."

"*Muy bien.* I'll go there now, and look around while I wait." They were almost at the exit, and Zara thrust her arms into the air in triumph.

"Oh, Jesus," said Dave as they passed through the revolving glass doors. "Here we go again."

"Sorry, Thunder Boy. I have to meet this lady before eight o'clock. Go check us in, and I'll be there as soon as I'm done, okay?"

Dave shook his head in surrender. "Okay, but I warn you. Acquire any more derelict properties, and I'll have to tie you up."

Zara's eyes lit up. "Promises, promises." She sidled up behind him and stroked his tight, jean-clad butt, pressing her body against his. "If I don't swing this deal, I deserve to be tied up. Do I get to choose? Leather, or handcuffs?"

Dave's mouth quirked as if visualizing the alternatives, and weighing the merits of each. "Gentleman's choice."

The humidity outdoors struck Zara in the chest like a hammer. The usual sunny skies had turned hazy and reflected a sick, yellowish glow.

"Weird," Dave said. "Seems like a storm brewing."

*

"My *querida* is coming home," Marlena said as she tucked her cell phone into her purse and rolled over on the blanket. She propped her head up on one elbow.

Picnic dinners had become a habit of late, and the unusually warm December day sent a pleasant breeze across the park. She looked over at Ernesto, reclining on the blanket in a similar position. He wore a casual pair of slacks and a short sleeved cotton shirt. Several of the upper buttons were left undone, revealing more skin than he'd exposed in quite some time.

"*Esta bien,*" Ernesto replied. "That will make you happy, I know. And I'll be happy to have David back."

Marlena giggled. "*Si.* She asked me to tell you something next time I see you. She has no idea I've seen you every day since they left."

"Tell me what?"

"To get busy with the site preparation of El Mirador. She wants to start building."

Ernesto smiled. "She's in for a surprise, then. I take it David didn't let on what he's accomplished."

Marlena shook her head and sat up. "Do you want to go for a walk?"

"Good idea." Ernesto began gathering the picnic things, but out of the corner of his eye, followed the movement of Marlena's lithe body as she stood and brushed a few stray crumbs off her skirt. When she leaned over to fold up the blanket, he took a long gulp from his unfinished bottle of Perrier before looking away.

"This way?" he asked, pointing in the direction of the park's central fountain.

"Okay." They strolled together up the cobbled path, despite the falling dusk.

Neither spoke until they reached a grove of trees that arched overhead. "Marly, what will this mean for you, when El Mirador is transformed? Have you decided whether you want to stay?" Ernesto asked.

Marlena slowed to a stop. "I haven't. If Zara needs me, I will stay. But there are things to be done back home. Bills to be paid, appointments to keep. I have guests invited for Christmas."

Damn. He felt no closer to gaining a commitment from her either way. He thought the time they'd spent together recently had made her consider certain possibilities. It seemed so obvious. Stay here, start a renewed chapter in her life. With him. "I understand. And after that?"

She looked at him with an expression of frustration. "I don't know. What is it you want me to say?"

Ernesto felt steel forming in his spine. If she wouldn't speak her mind now, she never would. It was up to him. Is that how Tristan captured her? Being forceful and controlling? Worth a try. He moved in close, placing his hands on her shoulders. He maneuvered her toward the sturdy trunk of a black oak. Her back met the rough bark, and he held her firm against it, moving one hand down to her waist, and placing the other flat against the tree, framing her in.

"Say you'll stay." His lips came within millimeters of hers, their noses brushing. "Say you'll marry me." He held her eyes captive, not allowing her to look away. They seemed to expand, become luminous. So beautiful, he thought his heart might burst if they broke contact. So he refused let it happen. He consumed her mouth with his own, his skin rough and hot against hers cool and tender. He slid his hand up to her breast, his thumb grazing the nipple through the sheer fabric of her blouse.

Marlena twitched and stiffened, trapped between him and the tree trunk. A soft grunt echoed from her throat. He kissed her harder, unrelenting, until he felt her acquiesce. He pressed his whole body against hers, making her acknowledge his need, then pulled his lips away just enough to whisper. "Say it, Marly. You know this is right."

The sight of her pert bosoms moving up and down with each anxious breath she took nearly drove him mad. "Ernesto," she gasped. "Make love to me…please."

Chapter Twenty-Four

Dave opened the doors to the balcony of their hotel suite. The air conditioning seemed to have failed, leaving the room in a tight, stuffy state. He stepped out, hoping for a cleansing breeze to alleviate the stifling atmosphere. No luck. The yellow-tinged clouds hunkered overhead, sucking the very life from the streets of Puerto de la Cruz.

In the courtyard below, the swimming pool offered a blue oasis amid the gloom. He watched some children splashing about in it, riding colorful foam noodles and tossing beach balls across its surface. Their parents lounged on padded deck chairs nearby. He pictured himself among them, stealing vigilant glances at the little ones from behind magazine pages, ever watchful. The hubbub of delighted squeals and carefree laughter floated up to him, making him smile. A new and different kind of life lay ahead of him. He couldn't wait to show Zara the progress on the El Mirador site.

Turning back inside the room, he decided to take a shower while he waited for her return. He reached for the house phone to make a dinner reservation for later, one he planned would be the most romantic and extravagant in history.

*

Zara gathered her hair behind her head with both hands. The wind had picked up enormous velocity and seemed to come from all directions at once. She tied it in a makeshift knot to keep at least the longest strands out of her face. She checked her watch, and re-set it to local time. Nearly seven o'clock. The estate agent had better show up soon, or the deal might be lost. Los Tiedes, as she decided to call it, stood resolute on its scrap of beach just ahead, ugly and desolate as before. Its conical roof jutted into the gray sky, the light passing through its missing windows forming rectangular eyes that seemed to glow dully at her.

"You will be fantastic!" she shouted at the abandoned walls. "My father said so." That constituted an anointment, of sorts, one Zara swore to uphold. A drop of rain struck her face. She looked upward, noting the heavy clouds had sunk lower and taken on a darker, more menacing hue. She clutched her sweater about herself, and stepped closer to the building. The roof seemed more or less intact. If it did start to rain, it looked safe enough to stand under.

It took only moments for the fat, random raindrops to accelerate into a steady patter. A low rumble reverberated from the temperamental sky, and Zara found herself at the entrance to the structure, hiding under its shallow overhang. At least a hundred meters of open sand stretched between Los Tiedes and the nearest building.

The rain increased to a pelting onslaught, driving sideways so that even the roof overhang afforded no shelter. Zara turned her back to it, and faced the open maw of the old restaurant. The sign with its faded red letters swung loose in the wind. When her shoulders were soaked through with wetness, she stepped inside.

The place smelled of rotting wood, mingled with the scent of new rain pushing in from outside. The floorboards were missing in several places. She stepped carefully around the open holes to a stable area near one wall. A dull flash of lightning illuminated the windows for a split-second then went dark again. The rain drummed a frantic rhythm on the roof. She told herself it would pass in a few minutes, and she might as well make herself comfortable. She dropped her red handbag onto the weathered planks and sat down cross-legged next to it.

And waited.

Lightning flashed again. She counted, like she did as a child, the number of seconds between the lightning and the thunderclap, each second equaling one mile distant. One-one thousand, Two-one thousand...Crack! Rumble, rumble. *Two miles.*

The wind howled through the openings, dropping the temperature, but failing to ease the cloying humidity. She hugged her knees and put her head down, condensing herself into a tight ball.

Another flash. One-one thousand, Crack! Way louder this time. The wall she leaned against shook and buckled, and she heard a tinkling remnant of glass falling from the windowpanes on the upper floor. *Shit.* Not a good place to be. Darkness set in at a rapid pace, her surroundings taking on a surreal and sinister cast. She bit her lip, willing the storm to abate.

She began to hyperventilate, inhaling and exhaling in short, frequent bursts. Considering its sudden arrival, perhaps the storm would depart just as quickly. She clung to this thought, rocking back and forth on her rump on the rough wooden floor.

Another brilliant flash illuminated the space, the millisecond of light throwing sharp shadows off the irregular, crumbling interior. Zara closed her eyes, the vestigial image of broken wall panels leaving a ghostly face to linger in her mind. Crack! The deafening thunderclap made her jump. Not even a count of one. The storm hovered directly overhead.

Her nostrils tingled. The musty air became overcharged with a sharper, stranger odor. On reflex, she shot to her feet, and propelled herself to the doorway. The arched entrance lit up with the next bolt of lightning before she could get even one foot across it. The teetering wooden sign broke free and blew away with the wind. She tumbled out onto the surrounding beach, her ears filled with the hideous sound and smell of splintering, burning wood. She crawled and scrambled toward the water, when something whacked across the back of her neck and made her see stars. She felt about to vomit before her vision faded to black.

*

His text messages went unanswered. Nearly two hours had passed since they'd parted ways at the airport, and the skies roiled and sparked with the oncoming storm. Dave couldn't wait any longer. He laced up his running shoes and left the hotel, striking out along the Playa toward the site of El Pescadore, or whatever she called it.

He passed the bars and restaurants, souvenir shops and market stalls, away from the lighted, paved walkways. No vendors lined the strand hawking their paintings and jewelry at this time of night. He picked up his pace, running almost full out into the darkness beyond. Lightning ripped the sky in jagged scratches. He hadn't seen this kind of storm since he'd left Thunder Bay, and knew better than to be out in the open in such weather activity. But it didn't stop him. Zara might be out there in the dark.

After about ten minutes, he could make out the shape of the old building in the distance with the help of intermittent lightning blasts. Rain pelted down, hitting him in the face and shoulders. The sand squelched beneath his feet, making running more difficult. Thunder rumbled in the wake of the lightning, the wind pushing the rain nearly horizontal against him. He closed the distance between himself and the cylindrical structure, to within about 100 meters, when a horrific bolt of lightning reached down its blinding-white tentacles and struck its conical spire.

Along with an earthshaking roll of thunder came a screeching sound unlike anything he'd heard before. Smoke began to rise from the roof of the building, and Dave flattened himself on the wet sand, waiting for the next strike. He kept an eye on the roof line, while gaining a sense of which direction the storm might be traveling before getting up again. It appeared to be moving to the south, and he took off at a dead sprint toward the smoldering shack.

Like a bad movie, the distance between him and his destination seemed to stretch and expand the faster he ran. Fifty meters, forty, thirty. When he reached the ten meter mark, he could see torn wooden boards hanging over the empty entrance at crazy angles. The whole affair seemed to be self-destructing, loose siding hanging from its walls as if it were shedding its skin. Sparks flared from the roof and sputtered in the drenching rain. The smell of singed wood carried across the beach on wisps of smoke.

He saw no other motion on the near side of the thing, so as he slowed his pace, he veered left to circle the building and scan its perimeter. He could see the angry surf crashing against the sand on the seaward side, the breakers reflecting what dull light remained. The beach appeared as an indistinct band of grey. A flash of lighting, dimmed by cloud cover, spread a temporary brightness over the area. Enough to reveal a rounded shape plastered to the sand by the driving rain.

A body.

Dave blocked all the thoughts that clamored for attention in his brain, refusing to let an irrational conclusion spring forward from the din. He let all sound drop from his consciousness, focusing on accelerating his strides to reach the sodden form. He almost didn't want to know, willing it to be some unknown person who'd fallen down drunk in the storm. The body lay on its side, and he dropped to his knees beside it.

He recognized the material of Zara's sweater.

Oh, God, no!

He gritted his teeth, and placing his shaking hands on her shoulder, rolled her onto her back across his lap. Her left arm flopped toward him. Soaking wet strands of hair stuck to her face, covering the bridge of her nose and the tip of her chin. Her eyes were closed, and he felt something leave his body in a baleful howl. His nightmare had just become reality. Worse than that, because there were two lives at stake now.

A chilling gush of water swept over them as she lay unmoving in his arms, soaking them to the skin before fleeing back from whence it came. Bits of seaweed clung to her hair, and he brushed it away from her face while shielding her from the pelting rain.

"Zara!" he shouted over the cacophony of breaking surf, hammering raindrops, and rumbling thunder. "Zara!" He stroked her forehead, her cheeks, her chin. In his dream, she'd always been alive before the lightning flash. Then afterward, her eyes would freeze open and she would slip away from him somehow. And always, the dolphin mocked him. Then he realized that none of these conditions were present. In fact, they were the opposite. Her eyes lay closed, he held her tight in his grasp and no ghastly metal creature hung around her neck. *The outcome could be changed.*

He hoisted her upward, and over one shoulder, intending to haul her away bodily. As he pushed to his feet, she coughed and spat water. Dave's heart did a joyous flip.

"Damn you, must you always scare the living hell out of me?" he shouted. Her feet kicked weakly, and he slid her down to land on her toes, keeping her tight against him. He framed her face with both hands, and looked into her green eyes that sparkled with life, not pale death. "Now, you literally are Lightning Girl. When will you ever listen to me?"

Zara's lips trembled as the rain splattered her face. "When will you ever stop rescuing me?" Her voice sounded choked and thin. She licked away the drops that kept rolling into her mouth. "I—I guess you'll have to tie me up."

"Yeah, I'll tie you up, all right," he said, pressing her face to his chest and cradling the back of her head. They had to get out of the rain and the ruined Pescadore offered the only shelter available. Dave herded them both under its ripped and sagging roof.

As the storm moved off, the rain settled to a calmer, steady drumming overhead. Dave moved to the driest part of the interior, and sat them both down on the wooden floor. The red bag lay on its side nearby, its contents partially spilled.

"I can't take much more of this, babe. No more abandoned buildings, okay!" His voice came off angrier than he'd meant. "Are you hurt? And don't say 'I'm fine.' Because you're going to a hospital either way." He removed his shirt, using it to wipe away the wet and sand from her arms and face as he examined her. No cuts or wounds were visible in the inadequate light. "Wasn't someone meeting you here? What the hell happened?"

Zara coughed. "The estate agent was supposed to…" She spotted her cellphone amid the pile of junk from her purse. "My phone," she said, pointing. Dave leaned over to retrieve it.

She took it from him with wobbly hands and thumbed its keypad.

"No signal. They couldn't even call me." She dropped her hands in her lap. "No one showed."

Dave sighed. "Well, we have to get you out of here. I want you checked over. No arguments," he said, and began scooping up the littered bits into her red bag. "This damn thing," he said, tugging on the shoulder strap, "Is the luckiest piece of shit ever. I think it would survive a nuclear meltdown."

Zara started to laugh, then sucked air in rapid breaths. She seemed paler than the thin moonlight that had begun to emerge from behind the clouds. Instinct told Dave that something was horribly wrong. He scrambled over to her, just as they heard shouts from outside and footsteps on the wet sand. Narrow beams of light began to flash and undulate toward them.

"Senorita Flynn?" a woman's voice called. "It's Roberta, are you in there?"

Zara bowed her head, as if in total fatigue. "Hurts…" she said, before tilting sideways and slumping toward the floor. Dave grabbed her.

"In here!" he shouted as the bouncing flashlight found the opening to the place. Roberta and another man stood in the entrance. "Call an ambulance," Dave said as he slipped an arm under Zara's legs and eased her flat onto the floor.

"Call 911," Roberta said to the man accompanying her. She turned to the pair huddled inside. "I'm Roberta Diaz, from Isla Real Estate. I'm so sorry, the storm came up without warning. Is she all right?"

"I don't think so," Dave said. In the beam of Roberta's flashlight, he saw his arm coated with blood.

Chapter Twenty-Five

Zara smiled as she watched the carousel spin and spin. The summer air seemed to sparkle and shimmer all around. Excited carnival sounds reverberated in her ears, the sounds of children's laughter and calliopes, bells and firecrackers.

The pretty, painted horses cantered up and down on their metal poles as the carousel turned, their faces frozen in pony-grimaces. But where were the children? Not a single one rode on their bejeweled backs. She stopped smiling. There were no children, no people at all, at this carnival. The carousel slowed, and the music seemed to bend and fall out of tune.

The scene faded to white, leaving only the echoes of the disjointed melody in her head. She opened her eyes to a room equally white. Boring, standard ceiling panels connected to pale walls devoid of any decoration. Moving her head, she took in more of the scenery, which consisted of a TV, a radiator, a window, an IV stand and small night table. Turning the other way brought a better view. A sleeping Dave sat in an armchair next to her bed, one arm draped over the side and the other propping his head up with his fist. His brown hair fell across his face in street-gang fashion.

He'd said he would take her to a hospital, but this seemed excessive. Her gaze fell on the thin plastic tubing running from the hanging IV bag, and followed it to where it connected. *Good Lord. I'm hooked up.* Her foot kicked out from under the sheet and bumped the metal stand. The noise woke Dave up. He raised his head, and inhaled a long breath. Then he jerked upright, tossed the hair out of his eyes, and stared at her.

"Babe," he said. "Thank God…you're back. How are you feeling?" He rose from the chair and leaned his hands on the edge of the bed. He looked tired, dark hollows forming beneath his eyes. "I was so worried."

Zara blinked a few times. "You worry too much, Thunder Boy. How long have I been here?" she asked.

"Since last night. Do you remember anything?"

She thought about it. "I remember the storm. I remember you and I sitting inside…Los Tiedes." She gulped in disappointment. The building she'd hoped to buy was beyond salvaging at any cost, now.

"Los Tiedes?" Dave questioned. "I thought it was 'Pescadore' ".

"That's what Dad called his drawing," she said, frowning. "What's the deal? Did I break something?" She checked under the covers. No broken leg, not even a bandage.

Dave bit his lip. "You lost a lot of blood."

"I did? I don't see—" She broke off upon seeing his expression. His handsome face twisted oddly, his dimples contorting as he looked away, struggling to fight back his emotions. More memories coalesced in her mind. Pain. Blurred images of flashing red lights. A medical crest on the sleeve of someone bent over her.

"My baby," she whispered hoarsely.

He turned his face back to her, his cobalt-blue eyes drowning in tears. He shook his head. "No. Not any more."

*

Jorge panned the good-sized studio, noting the placement of light fixtures and electrical outlets. Once the fittings were installed and the décor staged, it would make a very chic salon. A good investment. At least, Ivette hoped he would think so.

She hadn't imagined taking on a business partner. With Carlos' backing, she wouldn't have seen it as a partnership in the commercial sense. At least she knew what Carlos would have expected from the deal. Not knowing him from Adam, she wasn't entirely sure what Jorge had in mind, but he'd insisted on seeing the space.

He toured around the large loft one more time, checking the windows and doors. Finally he stood with his hands in his pockets, nodding. "It's a good location. You should get many high-end clients. And you could market yourself in the building. Offer specials to employees."

Ivette wrinkled her brow. He sounded as if dictating a business plan. She hadn't asked for that. Suddenly she worried what else he might want in return for helping her out, but he didn't seem the type for blackmail.

"Senor Allesandro," she said. "I don't need any help running the business. I know my trade. And I'm flattered that you want to help me. Shocked, in fact." She paused, and cleared her throat. "But there must be something you want out of this. You should tell me now, so that we…understand each other."

Jorge tilted his head. "Understand each other? I think you give me too much credit. It's not *complicado*. And call me Jorge."

Ivette spread her hands wide. "Well then, Jorge. What is it? I think you're a nice person, but nice people don't go around offering money to strangers."

Jorge looked up at the ceiling. "I expect…" He paused in thought. "I expect, haircuts for life. And one spa treatment per week for my mother."

Ivette's eyebrows raised. "That can't be all. How do I pay back the front money?"

"You don't. It's a gift. You see, I recently discovered I own a bit of property myself. I won't need much to live on, and I have no children." He turned his face back to her. "Do you have children?" he said suddenly, as if embarrassed he hadn't asked the question before.

Ivette smiled. There truly were good people on this earth, and at that moment, she realized something. That she couldn't continue to hurt an equally good person. He deserved better. She shook her head in reply. "Not quite yet."

*

Pam hesitated at the door to Vanier's room. She really had no business on this ward, but promised Zara she'd monitor his condition. And as much as she couldn't explain it, she felt something around this guy. Guilt? No. He'd called her 'Tonto', for God's sake. Satisfaction? At seeing him punished for his arrogance and for the way he'd hurt Zara? Maybe a little. Or something else? She pushed the door open.

He lay there dozing, the white hospital sheet in disarray overtop him. One foot hung out over the edge of the bed, and his chest lay exposed. His bare, hairy, perfect chest. *Whoa, where did that thought come from?* Mr. Arrogant apparently did not deign to wear a gown. His nurses probably wouldn't complain though if what she saw so far was any indication of what else might be hidden under that rumpled cotton. She stepped closer to the bed.

Here lay an impressive specimen. The telltale bulges and curves of his body couldn't be missed by even the most casual observer. He'd looked good in a suit, but lying here in the raw…holy shit. Pam whistled.

He moved his wounded head a little at the sound. Pam clapped a hand to her mouth. Waking up patients with head injuries wasn't smart. She prayed he'd fall back asleep. With his hair partly shorn away, she could appreciate the classic lines of his face. He looked a bit like Robert Redford, she thought. In his day.

He stopped moving, but his eyelids lifted to reveal a pair of hazel irises, their tone clear and rich, like vintage scotch whiskey. They stared at her for quite some time, making Pam's feet feel rooted to the floor in a tingling paralysis. His mouth began to twitch as if he wanted to speak. As he slowly licked the dry, cracked skin of his lips, something did a quick dance in Pam's stomach. A helpless, bandaged man in a hospital bed had no right to look that sexy. She scolded herself internally.

"Well, look who's here. Aren't we in a pickle now?" he said, his voice thick.

Pam swivelled her head and gave him a sideways glance. She raised her fingers in the air, mimicking two pistols. "What do you mean, 'we,' paleface?"

His parched lips curled into a smile, and issued a short, tortured laugh. He raised his hands to his chest. "Ooh, got me."

Her hands returned to the pockets of her scrubs. "Serves you right."

"What are you doing here?"

"I work here."

He turned his head away and looked up at the ceiling. "My luck."

"Yeah, you are lucky. You could be dead. But you seem not much worse for wear. What does your doctor say?"

Stephane sighed. "The consensus seems to be, if I weren't such a big, thick-headed brute I'd be in a lot worse shape."

"Mmm." Pam nodded. "So there's no truth to the 'bigger they are, harder they fall,' axiom?"

He turned to look at her again. "You're funny." The hazel eyes moved up and down her five-foot-nothing frame. "How much do they pay you here?"

She folded her arms across her chest. "What the union tells them they must. Why?"

"I hate hospitals. I'm going to need some full-time home care for a while. I'll pay you double what you make here. What do you say?"

Pam's eyes nearly popped. "Are you nuts? What makes you think I'd work for you?"

He licked his lips again. "I'm sorry I called you Tonto. Horribly inaccurate and racist of me. It won't happen again. Now what do you say?"

Pam's mouth hung open, wrestling with how to respond to such an absurd proposition.

"Yes would be a good answer," he prompted.

She caught a glimpse of a powerful, hairy leg peeking out from beneath the sheet. She found herself wanting to snatch the material away and have a good look at what else he had to offer. Before she realized it, a word fell from her lips.

"Yes."

Chapter Twenty-Six

Dear David:
I hope this letter finds you well, and that you will
accept my deepest apologies for my behavior toward
you in the past weeks. You are a wonderful person
and I will always have warm feelings for you. I want
to thank you for your kindness and am sorry for the
trouble I have caused you.

I must tell you that you are not the father of my
child and that you have no legal or moral obligation
to him or her, or myself in the future. I acted out
of selfishness and fear, and regret involving you so
unfairly. I hope you can forgive me.

Sincerely, Ivette.

The letter had arrived at Dave's office a few days ago.
Zara folded the notepaper after reading through and mentally
translating the lines of Spanish for at least the tenth time. It
didn't seem to help.

After losing her baby, depression hung over Zara like a
cloud since their return from Tenerife. She'd stayed away
from work for more than a week, sequestering herself at

Club Marbella, resting, reading, or just staring out to sea. The letter's contents should have elated her, but instead seemed to deepen the sense of loss.

At her mother's urging, she agreed to come to the El Mirador site and find out just what sort of "surprise" Dave had alluded to ever since they'd left Montreal. Jorge pulled the Mercedes into the temporary parking lot created for the construction crews. At the far end of the lot, overlooking the build site, stood a trailer that served as a field office. Dressed in his usual jeans and work boots, Dave leaned against the wall of the trailer, awaiting her arrival.

The warm day found him wearing only his reflective yellow and orange safety vest on his upper body, revealing his muscled shoulders. In spite of the unfashionable attire, to Zara, he couldn't have looked more sexy.

He smiled as he approached the vehicle and opened the door for her. "Good morning, Lightning Girl," he said, reaching for her hand. "Glad you decided to come. Feeling better?"

Zara took his hand and stepped out of the car. "Yes. Now that I see you." They stared at each other for a few moments before he pulled her in for a kiss. She reveled in the sweet taste and texture of his lips and the sureness of feelings they communicated. God, she loved this man, and felt a renewed wave of sorrow wash over her that she no longer nurtured his seed inside her.

"Close your eyes," he said, breaking their kiss and tightening his grip on her hand. He led her to the trailer, guiding her blind steps across the distance and over the threshold. He maneuvered her into position in front of the windows. "Okay, open."

She opened her eyes, and beheld the wondrous vista below. Re-designed foundations ringed the oil sand field, their myriad tines of rebar thrusting upward, waiting to join the next sections of concrete. To the west, she could see footings and piles lodged into the hillside, waiting for additional structures to take shape upon them. Men, materials and equipment moved about in a symphony of activity, and beyond, the shimmering sea drummed its ancient, steady beat in time to it.

Zara's breath caught as she took in the scene. So much, in so short a time. They must have worked day and night to make this kind of progress. She felt like she'd been away from Spain forever and, at this moment, knew she never wanted to leave again.

"Oh, Mr. Parker, what have you been up to?"

"Mmm, look this way, boss." He turned her to the right, pointing her toward the full-color rendering of the finished villa and interpretive centre that hung on the wall.

Zara put a hand to her throat. She'd seen a lot of architectural drawings in her time, and none of them were as complete, as breathtaking, as clearly drawn from the heart as this one. She recognized the sweeping lines of her father's sketch, amplified with an inspired interpretation that transformed it from wistful concept to stunning reality. La Dulce Zara. She swore her own heart stopped beating at the sight of it.

"Do you like it, Lightning Girl?"

She spun around to face him, words and thoughts and feelings reeling about in her head. She nodded, her eyes searching his as if wishing to communicate the tumble of emotions telepathically. "Lightning Girl like. You drew this?"

Dave smiled his usual half-grin. "Didn't know I had it in me?"

Zara exhaled and shook her head lightly. "I do now. You're amazing." Without warning, she felt her eyes filling with tears. "Amazing," she repeated. "How can I…" Dave seemed to sense her imminent emotional meltdown and quickly pulled her to him. He kissed her with an intensity that seemed to draw the strength right out of her body. She wrapped her arms around his neck to keep from falling, and matched his heat. The rest of the world melted away.

A sharp rapping on the window brought reality crashing back. Ernesto stood there, wearing an amused smile and wagging a finger at them. They laughed, but obeyed his gesture that they should follow him outside.

The warmth of the Spanish sun welcomed them as they stepped out of the trailer and caught up to Ernesto. December on the Costa del Sol sure beat the hell out of Montreal. Marlena waited under a portable canopy a little further down the slope, and Zara giggled at the sight of her elegant, slender mother in a hardhat and steel-toed hikers.

"What's so funny?" Marlena asked as the three of them approached.

"Nothing, Mom." Zara waved off her laughter, but noted a small table under the canopy set with a bottle of champagne and four glasses. The edges of its white tablecloth flapped in the breeze. "What's up, Ernesto?"

Ernesto moved next to Marlena, and exchanged a knowing look with her. "A toast." He poured the champagne and passed around the glasses.

Zara's radar went up, and she glanced between them, looking for a clue. "To what?" Zara asked, accepting her champagne, but exasperated at the suspense.

"To the future. Your mother and I have some announcements." Ernesto put his arm around Marlena's shoulders and their champagne flutes clinked together. "First, I'm going to be away for awhile. So we'll be needing a new Operations Manager." He lifted his glass toward Dave. "David, are you willing to take on the job?"

Dave's eyebrows went up. "Uh, yeah," he said, turning to look at Zara. "Of course." He shrugged as if to say he was as surprised as she. "Hadn't you better ask the boss?"

Ernesto smiled. "I'm sure she'll agree."

Zara's radar zipped higher up the scale. "I do, but, this is awfully sudden. Where are you going?"

Ernesto looked at Marlena. "We're going back to Canada, together."

Zara stood as if frozen, her glass in her hand. "Together? You and Mom? What do you mean?"

Dave chuckled. "Like, together, permanently," he said, looking straight at Ernesto. "That's great, Ernie. Well done." He raised his glass, then tipped his other hand under Zara's wrist, pushing her glass into the air. "It's a toast, babe."

Zara's expression turned from dumbfounded to joyous. "I knew it! I knew there was something going on between you two. Oh, Mom, I'm so happy for you." She set down her glass and rushed over to Marlena, giving her a big hug. Then one for Ernesto. "Are you going to get married? Where will you live?"

"We won't decide any of that until the New Year," Ernesto said. "Your mother has obligations back home over Christmas. And, of course, the business won't run itself." He smiled. "We have all this to do." He waved his hand across the panorama of El Mirador.

Zara looked out once more on the busy site. She hadn't thought about how much extra work this put on Ernesto. The project would mean a lot of extra time; time he couldn't spend with her mother. As Operations Manager, Dave could take on the general foreman's role, especially since he'd masterminded the design. Ernesto deserved a bit of relaxation. A crazy thought leapt into her head. *Hmm. Maybe not so crazy.* "Ernesto," she said, "how's your French?"

Ernesto turned to her. "C'est bon, mademoiselle. Why do you ask?"

Zara took a deep breath in. "Well, there's an opening for President of the Board at the Montreal office. And I know this great condo in Westmount. Fully furnished."

Marlena and Ernesto looked at each other. Marlena's eyes did a humorous roll. "This day is full of surprises," she said.

"And it's not over yet." Dave took his cue to change the subject. "You haven't seen the best part." He set his glass down on the table, and took Zara by the hand. "Excuse us. We'll leave you two lovebirds alone."

"What now?' Zara asked as Dave led her further into the construction zone, stopping to pick up extra gear at one of the tool cribs.

"You have yet to see the best view of El Mirador." He fitted the bright reflective safety vest over her shoulders as they continued on to where a new crane had just been installed. Dave slid open the door to the man lift that would carry the crane operator up to the control platform. He bid her enter with a chivalrous swoop of his hand. *"Entrada, senorita."*

"Gracias, senor." She stepped into the lift's tiny cab, and Dave followed, closing the door and reaching for the controls.

"Hold on," he said as the hydraulics kicked in and the lift began to move. Zara grabbed a handrail and braced her booted feet. The scene took on an entirely different perspective as they gained altitude. The grand design of the whole site revealed itself, not just buildings, but pools and plantings, pathways and landscaping.

Dave stood close behind her, his arms around her waist and his chin on her shoulder. Rising meter by meter, the scope of the project changed and grew, and soon, some dark stonework became visible just beyond the site's perimeter.

"What's that?" she asked, pressing a finger against the glass.

"You'll see," he answered.

In a few seconds, more of the dark stone appeared, forming a pattern in the sand. It reminded Zara of a giant SOS on a desert island. But the thought stopped dead, when letters became legible from the pile of rocks and spelled out something else entirely.

MARRY ME, ZARA!

Her emotions got the better of her as they continued to ascend, and she began to cry. "Hey," Dave said, squeezing his arms tighter around her. "Is my spelling that bad?"

She made a choking noise. Sometimes his sense of humor made her laugh and cry at the same time, but this was no laughing matter. She desperately wanted to say yes, but her mouth seemed to have other ideas. "I can't."

He loosened his grip on her. "What do you mean, can't? Like, not today?"

She pressed her hands to the glass, staring at the stone letters becoming smaller as they rose higher. "No. I can't make you marry me out of pity. Or because you think you must after what happened."

"Why would you think that?"

Zara pounded on the glass. "Because I failed. Failed at the most basic thing."

Dave seemed at a loss to understand her. "What are you talking about?"

"I graduated at the top of my class. I made my own way in the world. I designed buildings, and tore them down again. I flew halfway around the world to take control of a corporation, and fought off those who wanted to destroy it." She bowed her head and her shoulders began to shake. "And I couldn't do this one simple thing. I couldn't carry your child. I'm so sorry."

He turned her around and gripped her arms with both hands, squeezing hard. She kept on crying, gasping for breath in between sobs. She clutched the mesh of his safety vest and twisted it in her fists, her anguish uncontrollable. He slammed the button to halt the lift, and they jolted to a stop nearly 100 feet in the air.

"That's it," he said roughly, next to tears himself. "We're going to get a few things straight between you and me. Right now." He put his hand under her chin and tilted her tear-streaked face toward him. "You are never to feel sorry about that, ever, got it?" She continued to sniff and blubber. "You are your father's daughter. But you are not him, got it?" She gave a tiny bob of her head. "Everybody can do something. But nobody can do everything, understand?" A tear dripped off the end of her nose as she nodded again. "We are going to build this place together. You told me, this was meant for us, remember?"

"I remember." She looked into his eyes, losing herself in their blue depths.

"So, you are going to marry me, got it?" *Was she hearing correctly?* "Got it?" he repeated. Her chin bobbed up and down one more time. "And we're going to fill this place with more children, as many as you want. Okay?"

Her tears stopped flowing. Every word rang like a bell in her head, each one louder than the next, until it sounded like the entire cathedral at Notre Dame.

He shook her gently. "Okay?" he said again.

"Okay."

He nodded, lowering his voice. "Okay. Have I made myself clear?"

"Very."

He cocked his head to one side. "I'm not so sure. I think I may have to make another business presentation." He leaned in close, brushing her cheek with his nose. Then with the tip of his tongue, began to lick the salty tears away from under her eyes. The unexpected move made Zara's body react in unholy fashion.

"Up here?" she questioned, her voice shaky. "Sounds risky."

"Safety first," he said, stepping back and positioning her body in the center of the lift's cab. "If nobody moves, nobody gets hurt." He reached into the pile of safety gear and pulled something out. "This should do the trick." Between his hands stretched a standard, construction safety harness. Under normal circumstances, it would be used to tether the crane operator when walking the boom.

Zara had a feeling these were not normal circumstances. She felt a hot blush rising under skin. Not just on her face, but on her belly, her thighs…everywhere, as she eyed the woven nylon straps and metal rings of the harness. The blue of his eyes turned a glittering sapphire, reflecting the same excitement already growing inside her. She'd enjoyed the drafting table incident, but this explored new territory altogether. "Is this standard safety procedure?" she asked, swallowing hard.

"It is now. Take your pants off."

Her jaw dropped in mock protest. "Hey, I thought I was the boss."

"Only on the ground, babe. Only on the ground. Now get 'em off before I rip them off."

Zara's hands went to the waistband of her work jeans and slowly did as requested. First the button, then the zipper. When she'd pushed the denim and panties past her hips and down to her ankles, she realized her boots were in the way. She straightened and looked at him, her lips in a pout and naked from the waist down. "Untie my shoes, Thunder Boy?"

He crouched down and removed her boots, tossing them over his shoulder. He pulled off the jeans, then lifted each of her feet in turn, slipping them into the loops of the harness. He pulled the contraption upward until the loops snugged around her bare thighs, then put each of her arms into the upper straps. Their eyes locked as he tightened the padded strips of nylon over her shoulders.

He fingered the buttons on her shirt. "These will have to go," he said, popping them one by one. "Safety hazard."

"Whatever you say." she replied, close to breathless. "You're the boss now." The shirt fell open, and he pushed the fabric aside to reveal her pink bra. Her chest heaved up and down with each breath, and her whole body tingled with anticipation. This dominant side of him intrigued her, drew her into a new arena of pleasure in which she found herself a more than willing participant. She would do anything he asked, and the knowledge that they were suspended high above the ground added to the thrill.

He traced the outline of her bra with one finger, examining it as if it were something foreign to him. "This is well-constructed. I see it has a breakaway, in case it gets…"—he pulled sharply on the front clasp until it snapped apart—"caught on something."

Zara flinched as the bra released, her breasts tumbling out with nothing to restrain them. Her nipples budded in the sudden rush of cool air. He tilted his head from side to side, an amused smile on his face, as if pondering his next move. Then he fastened the chest straps of the harness across her bosom, snapping the parachute clip in place with a click. The pressure of the strap compressed her breasts into two tight mounds. It seemed vaguely medieval, and it made Zara giggle.

From a toolbox, Dave brought out three large carabiners. He fastened two onto the rescue rings that protruded from each shoulder strap, the reached around her to clip one to the main ring in the center back of the harness. She felt him connect this one to something on the wall of the cab behind her, and realized she could no longer move forward or back. He attached two steel cables from the roof of the enclosure to the shoulder rings. Effectively immobilized in the tiny cab of the man lift, goosebumps rose on her flesh and her knees began to shake. It felt obscene, and delicious.

He stepped back and stood with his hands on his hips. He looked her up and down, as if admiring his work, then nodded in satisfaction. "I think that will do."

Zara wanted to speak, but found no words to describe her feelings at that moment. The sight of this man, about to do with her as he wanted, made her tremble with excitement. She could feel the blood pulsing between her legs, begging him to come nearer, touch her, ravage her. He moved toward her with aching slowness. She wanted him bad.

At last, he came close enough to take her face in his hands and tilt it upward to meet his. The look in his eyes yielded a seething mix of desire, love and pain. They belonged to each other now, physically and spiritually.

"The purpose of this demonstration," he said, "is to prove to you that I'm a man of my word. I said I would never hurt you, so I intend to bring you pleasure, in every way imaginable. Starting now. Deal?"

"Deal," she answered, hear voice little more than a squeak.

"I also said that I would never let you go, and that I would never risk putting you in danger ever again, agreed?"

"Agreed." *God, would he ever quit talking and make love to her?* The nearness of his body, his rough vest brushing against her bare skin while she stood here in semi-bondage was enough to make her howl with want.

"And that I vowed to tie you up to prevent that, if necessary, correct?"

She nodded within the confines of his hands around her jaw.

"Good. This concludes the audio portion of my presentation."

"Thank G—" she began when her words were smothered by his kiss. Strong and insistent, his lips conquered hers and eradicated all desire to speak. His tongue searched her mouth, leaving no corner undiscovered. Then he withdrew his tongue and moved his kisses down the outside of her throat and to the hollow of her neck. Zara threw her head back in abandon.

Her arms still free, she tangled her fingers in his hair as he worked his way down her torso. Pain and pleasure mingled together as tongue and lips and hands explored her tight breasts, her nipples straining beneath the harness strap. He continued his path down her tummy, pausing to entertain her navel with slow, circular swaths of his tongue.

She convulsed in spasms of ticklishness, the pull of the harness underscoring her powerlessness. When he reached her abdomen, he simply kissed the skin there and pressed his cheek to it for a moment, as if in silent mourning for their lost child. She wept in concert with him.

On his knees before her, he then lifted each of her legs and placed them over his shoulders, suspending her in midair with her pussy spread wide. She quivered in the sensation of helplessness, and the anticipation of his lips nuzzling her in that most sacred place. She crossed her ankles behind his neck and hung there, resigned to his will.

Dave raised his hands and pressed both thumbs to her crotch, spreading the outer lips and exposing her wet and ready sex. He massaged the swollen bud, nurturing that magic spot he'd found before, until she arched her back and cried for mercy.

"Please," she moaned. "Please…don't torture me. I want you, now."

"Patience," he said as he plunged both thumbs into her depths. His tongue stroked the throbbing tissues of her clit, bringing her to orgasm almost instantly. Pleasure filled her mind and body. Wave upon wave of ecstasy washed over her as if it would never stop, yet she wanted more, wanted his cock inside her.

His tongue pressed against her,until the tiny contractions ceased. He lapped up the remaining juices from her quaking flesh and gently lowered her feet to the floor. Only the harness prevented her from falling, her knees seeming to have lost all capacity to support her.

Dave stood, sliding his hands up her legs and caressing her bare bottom as he rose. He released the metal carabiners that held her in place, and she collapsed against him. He whispered into her ear as she lay her head on his shoulder.

"Have I made my point?" he asked.

She wiggled her head in what passed for a nod. "You are…a man of your word."

He stroked her hair with one hand, and held her firmly around the waist with the other. "Have I done everything I promised?"

"No."

"No? What's left?"

"We need to fill this place with children. Starting now."

"You think you're the boss again, do you?"

"Yes." Zara tugged at his belt. "Time to get *your* pants off, boss man."

Epilogue

Fourteen Months Later

Marlena held the newborn in her arms, her expression positively radiating grandmotherly pride. "Justin Flynn Parker," she said, rocking the sleeping babe while gazing into his tiny face. "I'll bet you can't wait to swing a hammer."

Zara laughed. "Did you say the same thing when I was born, Mom?" She watched her mother fawning over the infant. The fine blond hairs on his head shone in the sunlight.

"No." She smiled in reply, not lifting her eyes from the child. "I didn't have to. I already knew."

Both women laughed. Dave moved across the wide deck of the boat toward them, working his way through the crowd of friends and relatives that had come to help celebrate the birth of their son. "What's so funny? Are you worried he's going to be too much like me?"

"He's like both of you," Marlena replied. *"El nino Hermosa."* A beautiful child.

Dave sat down next to Zara and watched Marlena cuddle the baby. "One down, how many to go?" he asked her.

Zara threw him a worried glance. "I'm not a building supply store, honey. You can't just requisition a yard full of children."

"Who says?" he asked, putting his arm around her and kissing her behind her ear. "I'll place them on back-order, then." Zara rolled her eyes.

"Well, I wouldn't mind," Marlena said. "I can't wait to have more grandchildren, but Justin would be enough for me." She looked down at the little boy's face again and touched his perfect, pink nose with her index finger. His eyelids twitched in response, but he continued to slumber in his grandmother's arms. "I wish Tristan could meet him."

"Somehow, I think he already has," Zara said, placing a hand on her mother's shoulder. The deck listed sideways as the boat caught a swell. With the demands of the project and no permanent place to live, a yacht had been the perfect solution for Dave and Zara to begin their new life together. Moored just offshore, they could access the build site in minutes and admire its daily progress each night as the sun set. The boat afforded a different view of a reconstructed El Mirador, but it remained, as Zara's father had said, magnifico.

Jorge came to join them. "*Miran,*" he announced, pointing out to sea. *"Un delfín!"* They turned to look in the direction he indicated, just in time to see the shining, gray body of the dolphin breach into the air then disappear beneath the waves. Gleeful shouts came from several guests who'd caught sight of the animal. "It's late in the season," Jorge said. "Most have swam north by now. This one must have wanted to stay for the party."

Dave's eyes narrowed as he rose from his seat to get a better look. He strode across the deck toward where the animal had appeared.

"Jorge," Zara said. "Aunt Juliana looks so well. The spa treatments seem to be working wonders. When are we going to meet your mysterious business partner?"

Jorge crossed his arms and smiled. "Someday. But today is Justin's day. Go," he said, pointing after Dave. "Show him the dolphin. Show him the world."

Zara took Justin from her mother, and gave Jorge a wry grin before turning away. She carried her newborn son in the crook of her arm as she joined Dave standing near the bow. He looked out to sea with a worried expression.

"What's wrong, Thunder Boy?" she asked, sensing his agitation. The new family of three stood together in the warm spring splendor of the Mediterranean, watching the dancing waves. Dave bit his lip, not answering. Suddenly the dolphin surfaced one more time, its glistening head bobbing and pointed beak open in a chattered greeting. It flipped and thrust its tail in the air, wagging it up and down in a symbolic goodbye gesture. Then it vanished.

Dave watched for a few moments more then exhaled a lungful of air. It seemed to have departed for good. "Not a thing, babe. Everything's exactly right."

THE END

Other books by Jean Maxwell:

El Mirador
(Spanish Seduction 1)

Indecent Proposal
(Workplace Gone Wild Book 1)

The Witch Doctor
(Nine Lives Chronicles Book 1)

Winter Symphony
(Overtures Book 1)

COMING SOON

Incendio
(Spanish Seduction 3)

From the Author

Thank you for reading this book. I sincerely hope you enjoyed it, and if so, the favor of a customer review would be appreciated.

*

Stop by my official online hangouts and say hello!

idreamofjean.com
facebook.com/authorjeanmaxwell
@dearjeanmaxwell

*

Yours in words,

Jean Maxwell